The Haunted Mansion

From the Magic Kingdom to the Movies

JASON SURRELL

Forewords by Martin A. Sklar and Tom Fitzgerald

A WELCOME BOOK

EDITIONS

NEW YORK

This book is dedicated to my parents, Sandy and Dennis, for taking me on that first trip to Walt Disney World in 1975. And to Francis Xavier Atencio and the memory of Harriet Burns; Imagineers and Disney Legends, X and Harriet became my mentors and friends.

The author would also like to thank the following for their contributions to this book: X. Atencio and Rolly Crump; at the Walt Disney Photo Library: Andrea Recendez; at The Walt Disney Archives: Dave Smith and Robert Tieman; at *The Haunted Mansion*: Rick Baker, David Berenbaum, Patti Conklin, Stuart Fink, Don Hahn, Rhiannon Humes, Mona May, Rob Minkoff, John Myhre, Jay Redd, and Jennifer Tilly; at Walt Disney Imagineering: Tony Baxter, Patrick Brennan, Denise Brown, Alex Caruthers, Hugh Chitwood, Anne Clark, Dave Fisher, Tom Fitzgerald, Lori Gonzales, John Gritz, Cathy Harbin, Barbara Hastings, Kim Irvine, Eric Jacobson, Mike Jusko, Kathryn Klatt, Ralph Kline, Gary Landrum, Bernie Mosher, Diego Parras, Steve Pinedo, Katie Roser, Diane Scoglio, Theron Skees, Marty Sklar, John Solomon, Donna Sommers, Christine Tweedly, Mike West, and Don Winton; at The Walt Disney Studios: Andrew Gunn, Nina Jacobson, and Brigham Taylor.

Special thanks for their contributions go to: Greg Albrecht, Jess Allen, Patrick L. Alo, Jack Anastasia, Roberta Brubaker, Vickie Cameron, Holly Clark, Anne D'Arras, Julie Enzer, Bruce Gordon, Jonathan Heely, Ken Horii, John H. Kavelin, Joseph Kim, Danny Matsuda, Michael McGee, Anne Moebes, David Mumford, Paige Olson, Mark Rhodes, Ronald Robledo, Celine Salles, Lon Smart, and Patrick White.

PAGE 2: Sam McKim's official portrait of The Haunted Mansion, painted over a copy of Ken Anderson's original 1958 sketch.
PAGE 3: A billboard in the Southern California area announces the opening of The Haunted Mansion in 1969.

"Grim Grinning Ghosts" Words by F. Xavier Atencio. Music by Buddy Baker. © Wonderland Music Company, Inc. Lyrics used by permission.

Photograph on page 15 courtesy of the National Gallery of Art, Index of American Design.

Photograph on page 46 courtesy of The Historic Fourth Ward School Museum, Virginia City, Nevada.

Photographs on page 71, Music Room, and page 85, Bride's Boudoir, © Ph.Rolle/Disney. Photographs on page 64, Grand Staircase, and page 92, Singing Busts, © Sylvain Cambon/Disney.

For information address Disney Editions
114 Fifth Avenue, New York, New York 10011-5690.
www.disneyeditions.com
Editorial Director: Wendy Lefkon
Senior Editor: Jody Revenson

Produced by Welcome Enterprises, Inc.
6 West 18th Street, New York, New York 10011
www.welcomebooks.com
Project Director: H. Clark Wakabayashi
Production Assistants: Kate Shaw (1st edition);
   Amanda Webster (2nd edition)
Designer: Patricia Fabricant

Library of Congress Cataloging-in-Publication Data on File
ISBN 978-1-4231-1895-4

Printed in China
G559-1249-8-12214

Second Edition
10 9 8 7 6 5 4 3 2

FSC
www.fsc.org
MIX
Paper from
responsible sources
FSC® C005882

CONTENTS

FOREWORDS

EVERYTHING STARTS WITH THE STORY at Disney. So when I was asked one day in 1963 to write "real estate sign copy" inviting retired ghosts to take up new residence in Disneyland, I had to understand what Walt Disney had in mind for what years later would become the original Haunted Mansion.

It turns out that on a visit to the United Kingdom, Walt had mentioned to several reporters that one of the reasons for his trip was to search the old castles and country manor homes for ghosts . . . but only ghosts that had a passion to continue to practice their trade in a new environment, "built especially for them" at Disneyland. Walt's story became the inspiration for my sign copy, posted outside the completed exterior of The Haunted Mansion in 1963.

Walt Disney had actually begun concept work on a "ghost house" in the late 1950s and early 1960s when he turned loose Imagineering's master special-effects wizard, Yale Gracey, to "play." That meant Yale and Rolly Crump, especially, were free to experiment, to try out their wildest haunting ideas . . . to "play ghost," if you will. And they did, masterfully.

Pulled this way and that over the next few years, the staff of Walt Disney Imagineering was forced to let the stately (and unhaunted) building sit vacant along the banks of the Rivers of America in Frontierland for the next six years. Meanwhile, we presumed the ghosts and restless spirits attracted by my sign copy stood unnoticed in queue lines with other Disneyland guests, and joined them in asking over and over again: "When can we go into that magnificent Mansion?"

The rest is Disney theme park history. The Haunted Mansion, in many ways a tribute to Walt's enthusiasm (and his promise to the ghosts who took out those post-lifetime leases that "we'll take care of the outside if you [ghosts] take care of the inside"), became the first major attraction designed by the Imagineers after Walt Disney's passing. Today it is a classic in every Magic Kingdom park around the world. And whether you're listening in English, French, or Japanese, those Grim Grinning Ghosts will always "come out to socialize" when you ride a Doom Buggy through any of the Disney Haunted Mansions around the world.

MARTIN A. SKLAR
Executive Vice President
and Imagineering Ambassador
Walt Disney Imagineering

THE HAUNTED MANSION AND I GO WAY BACK, both personally and professionally. I remember when my parents took the family on our first trip to Disneyland in 1969, only months after the attraction welcomed its first guests. Having watched Walt Disney preview the show on *The Wonderful World of Color* years earlier, I'd been dying to get to Disneyland to see the Mansion in person. From the first ride, I was hooked!

Years later, I was fortunate enough to be hired as a "butler" at The Haunted Mansion at Walt Disney World. It was a ghoulishly delightful experience. I spent the entire summer ushering guests through the Florida attraction, then headed out to California to join the Imagineering team that had created the show to begin with.

Today, The Haunted Mansion still remains one of my all-time favorite Magic Kingdom attractions . . . and I'm not alone. Millions of guests around the world have been thrilled and delighted by Walt's chilling concept of a retirement home for 999 happy haunts. Yet as the Ghost Host is quick to remind us, "there's room for a thousand."

Even as I "ghostwrite" this, Imagineers are conjuring up new spirits and apparitions for the future. Perhaps a new character will materialize, bringing us to that even 1,000 ghosts. And don't be surprised if we build another Haunted Mansion in another Magic Kingdom somewhere, someday. After all, there are still a lot of restless spirits in the world!

Happy Hauntings!

TOM FITZGERALD
Executive Vice President,
Senior Creative Executive
Walt Disney Imagineering

Tom Fitzgerald (**LEFT**) and Martin A. Sklar

INTRODUCTION

WELCOME, FOOLISH MORTALS. You knew *that* was coming, didn't you? What better way to begin a trip through the history and mysteries of The Haunted Mansion than with that timeless greeting. I am your host, your—oh, you know the rest—and will guide your tour through the moldering sanctum of the spirit world, home to those infamous 999 happy haunts. They've been dying to meet you!

Walt Disney was no stranger to the dark side. From his very first Silly Symphony, *The Skeleton Dance* in 1929, Walt knew that fear was one of the most basic of human emotions. Memorable villains abound in great Disney animated films, from the Queen in *Snow White and the Seven Dwarfs* and Cinderella's wicked stepmother, Lady Tremaine, to *Peter Pan*'s Captain Hook and Maleficent in *Sleeping Beauty*. With such a time-honored tradition of thrills and chills, Walt wouldn't have approached Disneyland any differently.

The Haunted Mansion is one of the crown jewels of the Disney theme parks, a masterpiece of Imagineering, and a guest favorite since the opening of the Disneyland original in 1969. The old house on the hill is also the source of more misinformation and the subject of more urban legends than any other attraction. But, like any good ghost story, there is a fascinating truth behind this attraction, which lives in four different Disney theme parks on three continents in two hemispheres, and has metamorphosed into a frightfully funny film adaptation.

And now, prepare to enter the boundless realm of the supernatural. Kindly watch your step as you board, please, and heed this warning—the spirits will only appear if you remain quietly seated at all times. Oh, yes, and *No Flash Pictures*. Now, as they say, "look alive," and we'll start our little tour. There's no turning back now. . . .

OPPOSITE: Marc Davis's artwork adorns the infamous eye wallpaper in the Corridor of Doors.
BELOW: Concept art by Claude Coats.

First Story

IN THE MAGIC KINGDOM

Our Tour Begins Here

A "MICKEY MOUSE" OPERATION

THE ORIGIN OF THE HAUNTED MANSION dates back to 1951, four years before the opening of Disneyland and a full year before the birth of WED Enterprises (for Walter Elias Disney, later renamed Walt Disney Imagineering), the creative wizards behind The Walt Disney Company's parks and resorts. Walt's own less-than-magical experiences with his young daughters at neighborhood playgrounds and amusement parks and a lack of tourist-oriented attractions for visitors to Southern California at the time sparked the desire to create a place where parents and children could have fun together. Walt began brainstorming ideas for a "Mickey Mouse Park," to be located on an eleven-acre site across the street from his Burbank studio.

The tiny park was to include a Main Village, complete with a train encircling the park, a village green with bandstand, Town Hall, police and fire

PRECEDING SPREAD: 1968 concept art by Collin Campbell. **OPPOSITE:** Poster. **BELOW:** Harper Goff's 1951 concept drawing, "Church, Graveyard, and Haunted House," for Walt's proposed Mickey Mouse Park. **BOTTOM:** Goff's aerial view of the park.

departments, corner drugstore with soda fountain, opera house, movie theater, and other staples of small-town life. A nearby Western Village would be home to a general store, pony ring, and stagecoach rides. Other proposed areas included an old-fashioned farm and a carnival filled with midway games, roller coasters, and merry-go-rounds.

By 1951, Walt assigned studio art director Harper Goff (who designed the submarine *Nautilus* for *20,000 Leagues Under the Sea,* among other Disney icons) to create a series of sketches of Mickey Mouse Park. One of the first renderings contained a panoramic view entitled "Church, Graveyard, and Haunted House." The inspirational sketch depicted a ramshackle Victorian house on a hill overlooking an overgrown cemetery and a quaint, small-town church.

THE HAPPIEST PLACE ON EARTH

Walt's dreams quickly outgrew the initial, eleven-acre parcel, and he realized that conventional architects and conventional thinking were not going to be enough—he was going to need a full-time staff of creative artists and designers from his movie studio to make his dream a reality. And so, on December 16, 1952, Walt founded Walt Disney, Incorporated— quickly renamed WED Enterprises—to design and build Disneyland, and brought over longtime Disney animator and administrator Bill Cottrell to run it. This eventually became Walt Disney Imagineering, in 1986.

"There's really no secret to our approach," Walt said of WED. "We keep moving forward—opening up new doors and doing new things—because we're curious. And curiosity keeps leading us down new paths. We're always exploring and experimenting. We call it Imagineering, the blending of creative imagination with technical know-how."

In 1953, a new home was selected for the now renamed Disneyland in a 160-acre orange grove at the junction of Harbor Boulevard and the Santa Ana Freeway in Anaheim. That same year, art directors Richard Irvine and Marvin Davis joined Goff at WED to collaborate and expand on the design and planning of Disneyland. Walt saw the park as a unique opportunity to tell stories in three dimensions instead of two. The first Imagineers came from the motion-picture industry, and they applied the art and craft of filmmaking to the emerging concept of the theme park. Looking to Disney's animated features as source material, they storyboarded the new rides and attractions just as they would a motion picture. Walt even "performed" the rides from start to finish, just as he used to act out the plots of cartoon shorts and features for his artists. A new art form was born.

One of Marvin Davis's first assignments was to assist with the park's conceptualization, architectural design, and master planning. In early layouts for Main Street, U.S.A., the land contained a small residential area located behind the east side of Main Street. The small, crooked avenue "dead-ended" with a crumbling haunted house on a hill overlooking the turn-of-the-century Midwestern town. This area was eventually discarded and replaced by other planned "lands within a land," which included an International Street, Liberty Street, and Edison Square.

GO WEST, YOUNG MANSION

Disneyland opened on July 17, 1955, and, after a rocky start, became not only a smash hit but also a cultural institution. It was not long before Walt knew he would have to expand the capacity of The Happiest Place on Earth to allow for ever-increasing crowds.

As part of Disneyland's expansion, Walt resurrected his Haunted House concept in 1957 and assigned it to Ken Anderson, another top animator who had come over to WED from the studio. Ken had already proved his ability to combine fear with enjoyment as one of the lead designers on the Fantasyland dark rides based on animated features. These included Snow White's Scary Adventures and Mr. Toad's Wild Ride.

The old house's planned site had by now been relocated to the southwest corner of Frontierland on a site already occupied by Magnolia Park, a restful spot filled with shade trees, park benches, and a quaint bandstand, which provided a transition between the Swift Chicken Plantation Restaurant and Adventureland's Jungle Cruise. Walt planned to transform Magnolia Park and the surrounding area into a New Orleans–themed companion piece for Frontierland.

NEW ORLEANS: QUEEN OF THE DELTA

The Southern influence was nothing new to Frontierland. Aunt Jemima Pancake House (later to become the River Belle Terrace) featured graceful, wrought-iron balconies on its second floor. The Swift Chicken Plantation Restaurant, which sat a little further west on the banks of the Rivers of America, served Southern cuisine and was housed in a plantation-style mansion. Toward the end of the 1950s, Walt decided to make it official by adding a number of new attrac-tions, restaurants, and shops to transform this loose-knit area into a land of its own: New Orleans Square.

LEFT: A south elevation sketch of the Haunted House, created by Marvin Davis in 1961. **TOP:** Sam McKim's aerial view of the proposed New Orleans Square. The Haunted House can be seen in the upper left corner.

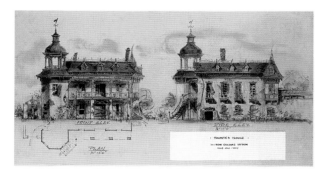

Walt went public with New Orleans Square in 1958, when the land first appeared on the Disneyland souvenir map. In addition to the restaurants, guests could expect a wax museum, a Thieves' Market, and, in the very center, a Haunted House. Walt mentioned the project during an interview with the BBC in London, as he expressed his sympathy for all of the ghosts that had been displaced from their ancestral homes due to the London blitz during World War II and new construction to make way for modern housing. He then announced that he planned to build a sort of retirement home at Disneyland for all of the world's homeless spirits. "The nature of being a ghost is that they have to perform, and therefore they need an audience," Walt said. Not even Walt knew it at the time, but the notion of a retirement home for ghosts would become a very important story many years later.

KEN ANDERSON'S FIXER-UPPER

Ken researched the great plantation houses of the Old South, in keeping with the period setting. However, the final design took most of its inspiration from the Shipley-Lydecker House in Baltimore, Maryland, pictured in a book of Victorian-era design found in the Walt Disney Imagineering Research Library. Other design influences likely included Stanton Hall in Natchez, Mississippi, and Evergreen House, a 48-room Baltimore mansion bequeathed to Johns Hopkins University in 1942, and now a public museum.

In 1958, while various story concepts were being considered, Ken drew a rough pencil sketch of a decaying antebellum mansion, complete with an overgrown landscape, sinister-looking trees dripping with Spanish moss, and bats circling in the dark clouds above. Fellow Imagineer Sam McKim took Ken's sketch and turned it into a painting that would become the attraction's official portrait. Everyone at WED was thrilled with the Haunted House's new look—except Walt. Even though the Haunted House had possessed an appropriately menacing appearance since Harper Goff's very first sketch in 1951, Walt didn't like the idea of a broken-down, ramshackle plantation house blighting the otherwise pristine look of Disneyland. The rendering led Walt to issue his famous decree: "We'll take care of the outside and let the ghosts take care of the inside."

Ken wisely decided to table the issue for the time being and focus his attention on the *inside* of the mansion.

GUNNING FOR INSPIRATION

In the midst of brainstorming ideas for the Haunted House, Ken made a fateful weekend trip to Northern California to tour the infamous Winchester Mystery House in San Jose. The sprawling, 160-room mansion had been built by Sarah Winchester, widow of the creator of the Winchester rifle, the "gun that won the West." Mrs. Winchester had been convinced by a psychic that continuous building would help her achieve immortality and protect herself from the spirits of those killed by her husband's creation. Sarah dutifully supervised the endless construction, creating a labyrinth of hallways and rooms of all shapes and sizes. Doors opened onto brick walls. Staircases led to nowhere, all to confuse the spirits from finding her. The sounds of hammers and saws were heard day and night, only silenced by Sarah's unplanned-for death thirty-eight years later.

Ken returned to Los Angeles convinced that he had found the perfect approach to Disneyland's developing Haunted House. Now all he needed was a good ghost story.

THE LEGEND OF CAPTAIN GORE

Ken wrote his first creative treatment in February 1957, setting the attraction inside the manor of an old sea captain, who, according to local legend, disappeared under mysterious circumstances many years earlier. A maid or butler character would lead a group of about forty guests into the house and assemble them on top of a moving platform that would take them down into the basement, where the actual tour would begin. The maid or butler guided the tour, pointing out secret passageways, changing portraits, and inanimate objects that came to life.

The tour began in a Picture Gallery, where another costumed servant met the guests. "Welcome to the old Gore Mansion," he would say. "I am Beauregard the Butler. Of course, it's not what it was around 1810 when Captain Bartholomew Gore brought his young bride here to live." In other drafts, the character was known as Captain Gideon Gorelieu, earning the nickname Captain Gore thanks to his bloodthirsty reputation. As Beauregard gestured to a portrait of Captain Gore, a pair of hairy hands would emerge from hidden panels in the walls and attempt to grab the butler—the first of many illusions and special effects.

In the next room, guests encountered the ghost of Captain Gore's ill-fated bride, Priscilla. Scenes such as these were designed like elaborate department-store window displays, illuminating and animating as guests entered, and fading to black as they moved into the next scene. The tour continued as guests watched Priscilla break into an old treasure chest that belonged to her husband, discovering to her horror that he was actually the notorious pirate, Black Bart. She screamed as the room plunged into pitch darkness. "No one knows what happened to Priscilla," Beauregard continued, "but she was never seen again—alive, that is. And after that ghastly night, Captain Gore knew no peace." It was believed that Captain Gore killed his young bride when she discovered his true identity and bricked her up in a cellar wall somewhere deep within the house. In subsequent drafts, Priscilla's fate differed—in one version the captain locked her body in a sea chest and threw the key down a well; in another he threw *her* down a well. Either way, Priscilla's spirit tormented him every night until he took his own life by hanging himself from the rafters in the attic.

As guests left the house, they passed by a crumbling old well. Scratched onto a nearby wall was a clue to Mrs. Gore's fate: "Ding dong dell, Priscilla's in the well. Who threw her in? The wicked cap-a-tain!" Guests peering into the well heard an ominous bubbling in the dark water far below as Beauregard the Butler offered a sinister parting thought: "And about the color of the water—maybe it's the reflection of the sun, but by an odd coincidence, it's blood red."

Concept drawings for a platform on which guests would be lowered to a room below.

BLOODMERE MANOR

In Ken Anderson's second version of the Haunted House story, written the following month, a guide welcomed guests to Bloodmere Manor, a hundred-year-old Southern mansion that had been moved in its entirety to Disneyland to be the cornerstone of New Orleans Square. An excerpt from Ken's second treatment explains the history:

> "This is the lakeside estate of the unfortunate Blood family. Our house had a tragic and bloody history of unlucky owners who died sudden and violent deaths, which resulted in their unhappy ghosts remaining behind to fulfill the uncompleted missions of their lives. We started the work of restoration as soon as it arrived at Disneyland, but strangely enough, the work of each day was destroyed during the night. It mysteriously remains always night within the house. So we recommend you stay close together during your visit, and please, above all, obey your guide's instructions. . . ."

According to Ken's story, the construction crew planned to completely restore the manor to its original Dixieland splendor but prankish spirits constantly undermined their efforts by breaking windows, trashing furniture, and smashing walls. One fateful day, a con-struction worker was accidentally walled up inside the manor. Work stopped immediately, and the old plantation house was left in its original condition. As the story continued, from that day forward the restless spirit of the doomed construction worker could "sometimes be heard hammering on the inside of the walls" of the manor.

WELCOME TO WALT'S PLACE

In August 1957, Ken came up with a most unique version of the story, with Walt Disney himself welcoming guests—live on tape. The guide was quickly dispatched by "a great hairy hand and arm." A playful "Lonesome Ghost" escorted guests through the house to discover its residents assembling for an elaborate wedding celebration. As guests peered down one dimly lit corridor, they would see the bride "lose her head" as her big day drew closer. "Did you ever see a lovelier sight?" the Lonesome Ghost would ask. "But she will have to pull herself together for the wedding." The story definitely had a lighter tone than the earlier tales of Captain Gore and Bloodmere Manor, but it still was not quite what Walt had had in mind.

THE HEADLESS HORSEMAN

September brought yet another version of the Haunted House story. Walt, "Hairy the Arm," and the Lonesome Ghost all returned, but Ken decided to return to his Fantasyland dark ride roots and look to Disney's animated features as source material for the attraction's climax. He found what he considered a natural: 1949's *The Adventures of Ichabod and Mr. Toad*, the inspiration for the beloved Mr. Toad's Wild Ride. Ken turned to the film's darker and much scarier second half, an adaptation of Washington Irving's *The Legend of Sleepy Hollow*.

The climax of this version of the show took place in the conservatory, which overlooked the graveyard behind the house. Then, according to Ken's treatment, *"The distant sound of pounding hoofs signals the approach of the Headless Horseman, who finally crosses the scene just outside the windows as his horse gallops through the tops of the trees."*

Many of the special effects in the scene were remarkably similar to those that would end up in the graveyard in the final version of The Haunted Mansion.

"The clouds will obscure the moon and distant flashes of lightning and sounds of thunder will next be heard. While the sky is darkening, the ghostly apparition of the Headless Horseman will fade into view or appear from behind a distant tree and gallop toward the graveyard and house from right to left foreground. He will disappear behind some trees to the left, but the sound of his horse's approaching hoofbeats will continue to grow louder. Suddenly, he bursts into view in the courtyard just outside the windows and gallops across from left to right, reining to a noisy halt just out of view below the balcony on our right. His cape is the only part of him we need to see at this last crossing, since the shrubs will

obscure the horse. His cape must match in color and value with the previous projected mirage. Next, a bolt of lightning against the sky and a werewolf's howl signal the appearance of the ghosts rising from the tombs, first one, and then two, and more, until ghosts are materializing from the earth around the tombs as well as the tombs themselves. Finally a blinding flash of lightning fills the room and dazzles the spectators, while a tremendous thunderclap ends the scene. The room illumination will increase at this point for the benefit of the spectators so they may see to exit."

The Headless Horseman's midnight arrival signaled the beginning of a wedding party, between "Monsieur Bogyman" and "Mlle. Vampire," and the conservatory would fill with a motley assortment of guests, including Dracula, Frankenstein, and Great Caesar's Ghost. The bride would plunge the celebration into chaos when she got cold feet and jilted the groom at the altar. As the show came to an end, a tour guide would manage to escort guests to the relative safety of New Orleans Square through a secret passageway in the fireplace.

OPPOSITE TOP AND BOTTOM: Ken Anderson concept drawings depicting vignettes for the Haunted House. Captain Gore and the Headless Horseman can both be seen, as well as a distinct voodoo influence that reflects the attraction's New Orleans setting. **TOP LEFT:** Ken Anderson plays with an all-too sinister doll house as he begins to mock-up scenes from his walk-through Haunted House. **ABOVE:** Ken Anderson concept sketch of the climactic appearance of the Headless Horseman in several incarnations of the attraction.

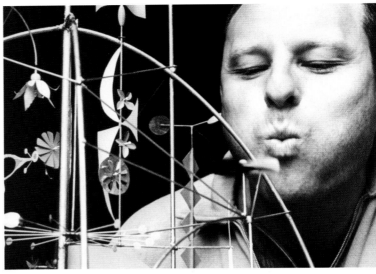

THE ART OF ILLUSIONEERING

With a story that everyone seemed to agree on finally in place, Ken and a team of fellow Imagineers took his concepts from page to stage in a series of mock-ups that began in October 1957. In early 1959, Walt recruited two more top artists from his studio, Rolly Crump and Yale Gracey, for the project. Walt knew that one of Rolly's boyhood hobbies had been magic, and the future Imagineer had taught himself how to re-create some of the world's most incredible stage illusions. Rolly was also well-known throughout the studio for his unusual mobiles, propellers, and other three-dimensional, moving objects he dubbed "kinetic sculptures," making him the perfect person to help tell Disneyland's three-dimensional stories. Yale was a background artist and layout designer who had a reputation as a mechanical genius and master model builder, creating models of experimental airplanes, trains, and other self-proclaimed "funny little things," exactly the kind of out-of-the-box thinking Walt looked for in his Imagineers. Recognizing Rolly and Yale as kindred spirits of sorts, Walt teamed them up and charged them with developing special effects and illusions for the Haunted House attraction.

Although Disneyland was and still is known for using state-of-art technology to tell its stories, many of the gags Rolly and Yale developed were inspired by some of the grand illusions and stage magic created by 19th-century magicians and from a book published in 1913 by *Popular Mechanics* entitled *The Boy Mechanic*. "The illusions Yale and I were perfecting were based on the 'black art boxes' and 'spirit cabinets' that had been used for many years by magicians," Rolly recounts. "We did a lot of stuff like that, always trying to carry the illusion a step further."

The two illusioneers spent most of 1959 holed up in a large room on the second floor of the Animation building. They dug out everything that had been developed for the Haunted House up to that time and used it as a springboard for new concepts and special effects. "We sat around and read ghost stories," Rolly says. "This is when Yale brought out the "Pepper's Ghost" idea [a deceptively simple lighting effect]. We started doing these little models to show Walt. We did all sorts of crazy stuff. We just played around with all kinds of stuff in that big room."

Rolly and Yale created and tested an entire mansion's worth of special effects, including gags in which it appeared that portraits and marble busts followed guests' every move, and an eerie projection illusion that would come to be known as the "Leota Effect." "Yale and I were roommates for the year of 1959," Rolly recalls. "Most of the stuff was his idea and I'd expand on it. Yale was kind of like a Geppetto, always tinkering with stuff. We were like a couple of kids just doing whatever we wanted to do."

Rolly relates one of the humorous side effects of their work. "Yale had all his ghosts and magic strewn throughout the room. Once, we got a call from personnel, asking us to leave the lights on because the janitors didn't want to come in if it was dark. Well, we did, but we rigged the room. We put in an infrared beam, and when it was tripped, the room went to black light and all the ghost effects came on. When we came in the next morning, all the effects were running and there was a broom lying in the center of the floor. Personnel called and said, 'You'll have to clean up your own room because the janitors won't go in there anymore.'"

THE MANSION RUNS A MOCK

At the end of 1959, Rolly and Yale staged their own mock-up of the attraction on one of the newly constructed sets for Walt's *Zorro* television series, resurrecting characters and story elements from one of Ken's earlier story lines. "We spent a year coming up with as many ideas, as much imagination, as we could," Rolly said in a 1993 interview with *Disney News*. "We made sketches and drawings and even little models of some of them. When we finally got more space to work in, we staged a full-scale illusion for Walt." In their demonstration, a murderous sea captain's ghost, covered with seaweed and dripping water from a tropical storm, appeared out of thin air. The ghost of his slain wife, whom the captain had bricked up behind a wall in this version of the story, materialized and flew toward him before both disappeared. "A ghost haunted by a ghost!" Rolly recalls, laughing. The captain dissolved into a pool of seawater, flooding the chamber. The water then dried up before the guests'

startled eyes, leaving only a few drops and puddles where he had been standing. Imagineers who were present have long claimed that the results were nothing short of spectacular.

Unfortunately for the Haunted House team, this scene (and presumably others like it) took anywhere from two to four minutes to stage, and Disneyland officials insisted that was much too long for an efficient operation. Walt wasn't sold on the show, either. It wasn't the story or special effects that concerned him; he wasn't sold on the idea of doing a walk-through attraction at all, having earlier been disappointed with the walking tour of Sleeping Beauty Castle. And to make matters worse, Walt *still* wasn't happy with the manor's run-down appearance, which had not been addressed. The combination of perpetual story problems, hit-or-miss special effects, and nagging operational concerns ultimately stalled the Haunted House project, which was put on indefinite hold.

OPPOSITE LEFT: Master "illusion-eer" Yale Gracey tinkers with a model of the It's A Small World show building for Disneyland.
OPPOSITE RIGHT: Self-professed "kinetic sculptor" Rolly Crump tries out a model of the Tour of the Four Winds he created for the 1964 New York World's Fair.
RIGHT: This concept sketch by Marc Davis of a murderous sea captain, a direct narrative descendant of one of Ken Anderson's proposed characters, eventually turned into a portrait for the Walt Disney World mansion.

All's "Fair" in Imagineering

THE SOUTH RISES AGAIN

THE HAUNTED HOUSE ROSE FROM the grave in 1961, along with New Orleans Square, both of which had first appeared on the Disneyland Souvenir Map back in 1958. However, the Magnolia Park home of the Haunted House had been taken over by an expansion of the Jungle Cruise attraction. With the Adventureland border shifting west, a small, horseshoe-shaped piece of land was designated for a new and improved New Orleans Square that would consist of a series of facades masking an enormous building containing the "Blue Bayou Mart." This would be home to the previously announced Thieves' Market shopping district, a restaurant overlooking a moonlit bayou, and, in the building's dimly lit basement, a walk-through Pirate Wax Museum. The site was far too small for the resurrected Haunted House concept, so Walt decided to move the attraction north to the site of the Swift Chicken Plantation restaurant.

A handbill passed out at Disneyland's Main Entrance announced that New Orleans Square and the renamed Haunted Mansion would open two years later in 1963. According to the handbill, "Gathering the world's greatest collection of ghosts is no easy task. Most people are kind of reluctant to admit they know any! But Walt Disney has had his talent scouts searching for several years . . . and in 1963 the Haunted Mansion will be filled with famous and infamous residents." Construction on New Orleans Square began in 1961, with The Haunted Mansion laying its foundations one year later.

Despite the best efforts of the Imagineers, the year 1963 materialized right on schedule but The Haunted Mansion was not quite as fortunate. The exterior was completed, but it was just the shell of a building with nothing inside. As built, the Mansion was a stately Southern plantation house that bore a striking resemblance to the one in Ken Anderson's original sketch, but without its ramshackle appearance. The Imagineers were indeed "taking care of the outside," just as Walt had directed.

Walt supplied another irresistible teaser to create excitement and build anticipation among guests. A sign penned by new Imagineering recruit Marty Sklar was posted outside the Mansion's wrought-iron fence soliciting spooks from around the world to take up residency in a ghostly retirement home.

However, The Haunted Mansion and New Orleans Square were both officially put on hold yet again as Walt turned all of WED's resources, including everyone on the Mansion team, to one of the grandest experiments and biggest gambles of his career—the 1964–1965 New York World's Fair.

Notice!
All Ghosts
And Restless Spirits

Post-lifetime leases are
now available in this

HAUNTED
MANSION

don't be left out in the sunshine! Enjoy active retirement in this country club atmosphere-the fashionable address for famous ghosts, ghosts trying to make a name for themselves…and ghosts afraid to live by themselves! Leases include License to scare the daylights out of guests visiting the Portrait Gallery, Museum of the Supernatural, graveyard and other happy haunting grounds. for reservations send resume of past experience to:
Ghost Relations Dept. Disneyland
Please! Do not apply in person.

OPPOSITE: Marty Sklar's infamous invitation to restless spirits from all over the world, erected outside an "empty" Haunted Mansion in 1963. ABOVE: A 1964 watercolor concept rendering of New Orleans Square by Herb Ryman. BELOW: A color diagram used to guide the painting of The Haunted Mansion, 1963. RIGHT: The Haunted Mansion's exterior under construction, circa 1963.

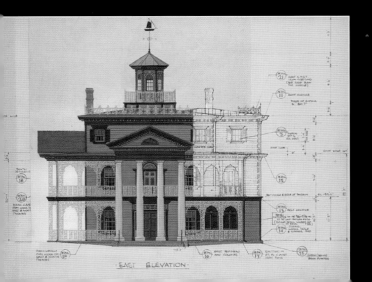

EAST ELEVATION.

NEW YORK, NEW YORK

With corporate support, Walt committed to building four attractions for the 1964–1965 New York World's Fair. The first, for the Ford Motor Company, was The Magic Skyway, a journey through the history of humankind, from the primeval world to the space age and beyond, aboard "real" Ford convertible automobiles. The second was General Electric's Progressland, a lighthearted look at the development of electricity and its effect on American home life, based on a show originally conceived for the abandoned Edison Square project at Disneyland. Great Moments with Mr. Lincoln was produced for the State of Illinois and the last project was a pavilion for Pepsi-Cola/UNICEF entitled It's A Small World, a musical cruise around the world starring hundreds of singing Audio-Animatronics children.

Walt's gamble paid off. The four Disney shows were the hits of the fair, and Disneyland subsequently received three brand-new attractions and a major addition to a fourth at very little cost. Great Moments with Mr. Lincoln took office in the Disneyland Opera House on Main Street. It's A Small World moved into Fantasyland, and the Carousel of Progress relocated from Progressland to become a centerpiece of the new Tomorrowland. Even the dinosaurs from the prehistoric segment of The Magic Skyway ride were used to create a Primeval World diorama on the Santa Fe & Disneyland Railroad. And the new technology developed would prove to be invaluable to WED.

Once the shows were completed for the fair, Walt and his Imagineers returned their attention to the projects that had been in the pipeline. Disneyland operators still maintained that any new attractions had to be "people-eaters," capable of accommodating not tens or hundreds but thousands of guests per hour. The Haunted Mansion was still slated to be a walk-through experience, but would also be a real people-eater, bringing groups of about forty people down into the walk-through area at a time. In a fashion similar to the construction of Pirates of the Caribbean, the bulk of the show would take place in a large, sound-stagelike building outside Disneyland's berm where there was more room, even though guests would still enter the attraction through the facade of the old Southern mansion that had been sitting in New Orleans Square since 1963. In order to meet the crowds Disneyland officials were expecting, Imagineers drew up plans for two identical walk-through experiences, each occupying half of one big show building.

THE THREE MOUSEKETEERS: MARC DAVIS, CLAUDE COATS, AND X. ATENCIO

Just as the show concept for The Haunted Mansion changed, a number of the players changed as well. Ken Anderson had gone back to the Studio when WED began to work on the fair, so Walt instead assigned animator and Imagineer Marc Davis and background artist Claude Coats to the project. After doing some design work for Disneyland on and off over the years, Marc had finally moved over to WED full-time in 1961. As one of Walt's Nine Old Men of animation and the lead artist on The Enchanted Tiki Room (Disney's first Audio-Animatronics show) and new Jungle Cruise scenes, Marc was a natural for the Audio-Animatronics spectacles that both Pirates of the Caribbean and The Haunted Mansion were rapidly shaping up to be. Marc would focus on creating the Mansion's ghostly characters and a variety of gags and scenes in which they could play.

In a treatment dated July 27, 1964, Marc developed his own take on the long-gestating attraction, replacing the Lonesome Ghost with a disembodied "Ghost Host" that would narrate a walking tour of the Mansion. The treatment also called for a live but silent butler character who would physically escort guests through scenes that included The Elongating Room, a clear forerunner of the Portrait Chamber, or Stretching Room; The Portrait Gallery, a room "filled with oversized furnishings, paintings and sculptures" and home of the "most dangerous ghost in the mansion," who "climbs out of his picture" to mingle with guests "until he has turned one of them into a ghost"; a Séance Room, home of "the famous medium Madame Z" (a full-bodied clairvoyant at that point); a Ghost Club Room, subtitled "A Meeting Place for Retired Ghosts," fulfilling Walt's original vision for the Mansion; and "A Room That Has

OPPOSITE: Walt Disney reviews Herb Ryman's concept renderings for The Magic Skyway, a ride-through attraction Ford Motor Company commissioned for the 1964 New York World's Fair. TOP: An X. Atencio concept rendering of a ghostly trio—only the organist survived. CENTER: The influence of Robert Wise's 1963 classic horror film The Haunting can be seen in this Marc Davis rendering of a corridor of doors. ABOVE: Marc Davis concept sketch depicting "the most dangerous ghost in the mansion" in the Portrait Gallery as described in his 1964 treatment. LEFT: The "Three Mouseketeers"—Marc Davis, Claude Coats, and X. Atencio—seen here reviewing character concepts for Country Bear Jamboree.

a Garden View"—"a room where great evil has taken place," the murder of a bride and her fiancé, according to the Ghost Host. Guests quickly discovered the "most dangerous ghost in the mansion" to be none other than the Ghost Host himself, who materializes from out of the rainstorm raging outside in shades of Rolly and Yale's 1959 mock-up. The Ghost Host then tells guests that it was in this very room that *he* murdered the young bride and her beloved, reviving still another original Ken Anderson story element. Guests are directed to safety through a secret panel in a bookshelf—by a talking raven.

Claude Coats, meanwhile, tapping into his experience as a background artist, would focus his attention on designing the Mansion's interior environments,

constructing lavish sets on which Marc's cast of characters could perform.

Animator X. Atencio came over to WED in 1965 as a scriptwriter. "Walt always had the knack of finding talents in his people that we didn't realize ourselves," X. told *Storyboard* magazine in 1989. X. had done storyboarding and worked in the story department, but had never done any scriptwriting. After he moved to WED and worked on Primeval World, Walt asked him to do the script for Pirates of the Caribbean. "I said to myself, 'I don't know anything about scriptwriting.' But I did the researching . . . and put on my pirate hat." X.'s work on Pirates would prove the fledgling writer a natural for The Haunted Mansion.

ABOVE: Marc's concept for "the famous medium Madame Z," a character that would eventually give way to the disembodied Madame Leota. BELOW: Marc Davis sketch of a mansion resident who literally loses her head.

OPPOSITE: Marc Davis concept sketch of one of the many merry minstrels that would eventually find a home in the Graveyard scene. TOP: Marc Davis rendering of a room that didn't make it into the attraction—the Kitchen—along with stage directions describing the otherworldly action. ABOVE: X.'s rendering of a ghost that "will follow you home," which helped inspire one of the attraction's most beloved special effects. BELOW: X. Atencio sketch of a gag that ultimately made its way into the Walt Disney World version of the attraction—minus the corpse (the spiderweb ultimately gave way to an Endless Staircase in the 2007 enhancement).

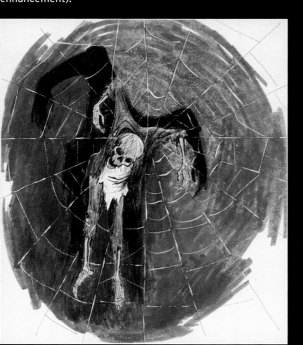

A WEIRD DIRECTION

Like he did with most everyone else at WED, Walt assigned Rolly Crump and Yale Gracey to work on the shows for the New York World's Fair. Unlike Ken Anderson, they returned to work on The Haunted Mansion after the fair, where they were joined by Marc Davis, Claude Coats, and X. Atencio, and all pitched their own versions of The Haunted Mansion to Walt. Rolly displayed sketches of a "candle man" with flames burning on his body and melting wax running down his chest, an otherworldly chair that stood up and chatted with guests, and man-eating plants chowing

down behind the glass walls of a conservatory.

"The concept of a haunted house was there from the beginning," Rolly told *Disney News*. "Some favored the 'old dark house' tradition of sliding panels, clutching hands, and so forth. Others saw it as a spoof, with lots of gags instead of scary stuff. I wanted to do something entirely different, something with a tremendous amount of fantasy."

Walt summed up everyone's reaction to Rolly's work: "This stuff is really weird, Rolly. What in the heck are we going to do with it?"

"I'm not sure, Walt," Rolly replied, perhaps a little too honestly, "but I feel that unless we put something in that's different, The Haunted Mansion is just going to be the same old thing."

Walt tracked down Rolly the next morning. "You son of a gun," he said, "that stuff drove me crazy all night long, but now I know how to use it." Walt then described an idea for the inside of the mansion's entrance—a spill area showcasing an unnerving display of oddities from all over the world. Guests could spend as much time as they wanted there, entering and exiting separately from the main show. This idea won out over such other concepts as a haunted restaurant, which would have been built into the attraction much like the Blue Bayou restaurant became part of Pirates of the Caribbean.

Rolly had submitted well over a hundred ideas for The Haunted Mansion since he had begun working on

the show in the late 1950s, and now he set about developing some of them for his new, Walt-christened "Museum of the Weird." One of the highlights was a freestanding gypsy wagon infested with spirits that would spring to life every few minutes. Doors swung open, bells rang, the wagon's contents flew around, torches burst into flames, canopies billowed, and a palmistry hand painted onto a side panel came to life.

Another plan was for a séance room with talking furniture, floating chandeliers, marble busts that followed guests' every move, and old family paintings that changed right before viewers' eyes. "The room would be filled with spirits," Rolly recalls, and he "worked very hard on a 'ghost host' concept" in an effort to link the museum to Marc Davis's evolving story line for the main show.

Though the Museum of the Weird went on to the happy haunting grounds in the sky when WED made the final decision to change The Haunted Mansion from a walking tour into a ride-through experience, many of the concepts and designs Rolly created made it into the attraction's final design.

OPPOSITE TOP, THIS PAGE ABOVE AND BELOW: In 1964 Rolly Crump created this series of renderings and sketches of characters and gags for his Museum of the Weird.
OPPOSITE BOTTOM: Rolly puts the finishing touches on a model for the museum. The Haunted Mansion model is visible in the background.

999 Happy Haunts

CREATIVE DIFFERENCES

ONSTRUCTION ON THE ATTRACTION stalled yet again in 1965, when Walt turned WED's attention to bringing the World's Fair shows back across the country for installation at Disneyland. Then two other projects managed to pull ahead of The Haunted Mansion. The first was the attraction's New Orleans Square sibling, Pirates of the Caribbean. The second was another redesign of Tomorrowland, which had stubbornly refused to keep as far ahead of the times as Walt wanted. But the biggest blow was yet to come.

On December 15, 1966, Walter Elias Disney died of lung cancer. Walt Disney Productions lost its founder and guiding creative force, the visionary who had the final say on everything that bore his name. And, in the case of The Haunted Mansion, the Imagineers at WED lost the one person who could break a tie.

Walt's death and the loss of his "final say" had a serious effect on The Haunted Mansion, which by now had been all over the creative map for ten years. Fortunately, Richard Irvine, now WED vice president of design, felt, with good reason, that there were two

master Imagineers who could guide The Haunted Mansion to completion.

The partnership of Marc Davis and Claude Coats had enjoyed enormous success on Pirates of the Caribbean, a testament to Walt's unerring knack for building a winning creative team. Walt knew that combining Marc's brilliant character designs and ingenious sight gags with Claude's strength in backgrounds, layout, and set design would produce greater results than any single artist working alone—a hallmark of Imagineering philosophy. Before his death, Walt had seen the results firsthand on their collaboration on Pirates, and Irvine expected their winning streak to continue.

The blockbuster success of Pirates, however, led both Marc and Claude to believe that each had earned a bit more autonomy and should be the one to take the creative lead on The Haunted Mansion. So instead of the winning partnership that produced Pirates, the final design of The Haunted Mansion was marked by creative tension between Marc and Claude. Their differences in approach also led to one of the greatest debates to ever take place at WED: should The Haunted Mansion be scary or funny? In one corner were Marc and those who felt that, ghosts being scary to begin with, the show should be lightened up. In the other corner, Claude and other equally vocal designers insisted that guests would expect some serious scares in something called The Haunted Mansion. Ultimately, Marc Davis was able to convince Dick Irvine to turn The Haunted Mansion into more of a comedy than a horror show.

Marc and Claude's creative differences resulted in two distinct experiences within the attraction. The first half of the show is all about the environment— a testament to Claude's experience as a background artist. It is a little more ominous and scarier, with nary a character in sight. The second half of the attraction, in particular the Grand Hall and the Graveyard, is less reliant on strong set design and filled to overflowing with Marc Davis's whimsical characters and sight gags. These conflicting approaches are among the reasons The Haunted Mansion doesn't have a linear story line such as Peter Pan's Flight or Splash Mountain. The show was turning into a motley collection of characters, scenes, sets, and special effects, and it would be up to show writer X. Atencio to make sense of it all.

OPPOSITE: Marc Davis's rendering of a knight who really loses his head. THIS PAGE: The seemingly divergent styles of Marc Davis and Claude Coats are evident in these concept renderings. ABOVE LEFT AND RIGHT: Marc's genius lay in broad characters and lighthearted gags, hallmarks of a master animator. BELOW, BOTTOM, AND RIGHT: Claude focused on creating moody environments and an ominous atmosphere, reflecting his many years as a background artist.

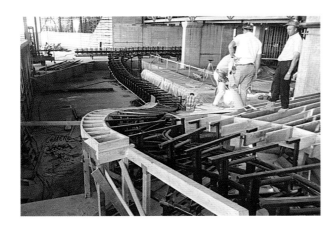

THE DOOM BUGGY

Another debate that still hadn't died was whether The Haunted Mansion should be a walk-through or ride-through attraction. Disneyland officials wanted to pump as many people through the attraction per hour as possible, and in their minds that meant a ride-through—especially after the success of the people-eating Pirates of the Caribbean. "Dick Nunis [director of Disneyland operations] was a bear for capacity," X. Atencio recalls. "We called him 'Hopalong Capacity.'" The Imagineers began looking for ways to make The Haunted Mansion a ride-through experience. Yale Gracey even worked on plans for a boat ride through an old plantation house partially submerged in a bayou.

The time-consuming delays and debates did have one positive side effect: by 1967, the perfect ride system solution was available. "Walt had just passed away as we started to work on the show again," Claude Coats told Imagineers Bruce Gordon and David Mumford in *The Nickel Tour*. "We had just finished up the Monsanto ride, Adventure thru Inner Space." The attraction featured a new and unique ride system called the Omnimover, a direct descendant of the WEDway PeopleMover developed for Ford's Magic Skyway at the New York World's Fair.

As it is told, one day in the mid-1960s, Bob Gurr, an Imagineer, was sitting in art director and Imagineering legend John Hench's office discussing what WED had learned from the fair. John happened to have a plastic apple sitting on his desk. Bob picked up the faux fruit and began to spin it completely around by the stem. Struck by the image, he remarked to John that they needed to develop a continuous chain-ride car that could rotate 360 degrees like the apple. Using the PeopleMover as a starting point, WED created the Omnimover.

The Omnimover consists of a train of swiveling, clamshell-shaped pods that can spin, turn, and tilt to point the guests in any direction, narrowly focusing their attention just as film directors do with their cameras. Guests would see exactly what the Imagineers wanted them to see, exactly when they wanted them

to see it. The new system would also allow Imagineers to send an endless stream of guests through the attraction at a constant rate, meeting Disneyland's capacity requirements and then some. WED copied Adventure thru Inner Space's clamshell pods, painted them black, and dubbed them "Doom Buggies."

The advent of the Omnimover, combined with advances in Audio-Animatronics led by master sculptor and Imagineer Blaine Gibson, mechanical geniuses Roger Broggie and Wathel Rogers, and programmer extraordinaire Bill Justice, led Imagineers to drop the concept of a walk-through for good in favor of a ride-through experience in which fully animated ghosts, ghouls, and goblins would share the stage with the illusions and special effects that Rolly Crump and Yale Gracey had been working on since the late 1950s. The switch sent some of the Imagineers back to the drawing board yet again. "Some of the gags and illusions that had been worked on by Yale Gracey were built with a walk-through in mind," X. Atencio told *Storyboard* magazine. "You would walk through, stop, see something happen, then you'd move on to the next set. When we finally decided it should be a ride-through, a lot of these things would not work; they would have to be repeating for every vehicle that goes through. One of the challenges in our rides is that you have no beginning and no end. These are illusions that are constantly in motion, and that changed the whole concept of the ride."

TOP: A rare view of Imagineers laying track during The Haunted Mansion's construction. **RIGHT:** The ultimate custom vehicle, seen here in WED's unique "body shop." **BELOW:** The Doom Buggies take a spin through the Corridor of Doors.

A Marc Davis concept rendering of some Grim Grinning Ghosts.

"GRIM GRINNING GHOSTS"

The success of Pirates of the Caribbean had a major influence on The Haunted Mansion's direction, from Dick Irvine's reunion of Marc Davis and Claude Coats to the attraction's conversion to a ride-through, but one more key element would not have existed without Pirates: a memorable theme song. More than one Imagineer had concerns about Pirates' potentially questionable subject matter, and it was X. who convinced Walt that a rousing song might be a good way to lighten things up a bit. "I thought he'd give it to the Sherman brothers," X. remembered. "I kind of half sang, half recited it, and Walt just said, 'Yeah, that's great, get with George (Bruns) to do the music.' That's how I became a songwriter." "Yo Ho (A Pirate's Life for Me)" helped the Imagineers turn a band of bloodthirsty cutthroats into more family-friendly, fun-loving swashbucklers.

X. took the same approach to Mansion as he did on Pirates, writing the lighthearted lyrics to "Grim Grinning Ghosts," alternatively titled "The Screaming Song," which were then set to music by veteran studio composer Buddy Baker. "When I did "Yo Ho," we couldn't have a beginning or an end, because you didn't know where you were going to come into the song in the ride. Each verse had to make some kind of sense, no matter when you heard it." Thus, the music cues are in perfect length and synchronization in each attraction to avoid an aural overload.

Not only would "Grim Grinning Ghosts" provide a musical backdrop for The Haunted Mansion's grand finale in the Graveyard, but different arrangements of the piece were used throughout the experience. From its first appearance as a funeral dirge in the Foyer to an elegant waltz in the Grand Hall to a jazzy jamboree in the Graveyard, "Grim Grinning Ghosts" helps set the scene and manipulate the listener's feelings each time it is heard. In order to make the Graveyard scene a true showstopper, X. and Buddy did everything they could to give those music cues an even more other-worldly quality, including detuning the instruments and recording the music backward and combining it all in the final mix.

LEFT: Sketch of ghostly ideas by Ken Anderson. **ABOVE:** X. Atencio, who had to make sense of more than ten years' worth of characters, stories, and special effects in his script for The Haunted Mansion.

THE END OF THE STORY

Show writer X. Atencio's main task after joining the team was to take Marc Davis's humorous characters and vignettes, Claude Coats's sinister settings, and Rolly Crump and Yale Gracey's haunting illusions and special effects and combine them in a way that made sense. "We tried at the beginning at having a raven be the Ghost Host that would take you through, but it didn't work." X. Atencio says. The raven's small size made it difficult to stage amid all the elaborate sets and eye-popping special effects—he kept getting lost in the chaos. X. quickly decided to drop him in favor of the simpler, disembodied Ghost Host who had appeared in a number of different treatments over the years. X. then took the scenes on which Marc and Claude were collaborating and arranged them logically in terms of the Mansion's physical layout and the experience's overall emotional construction. Almost by default, X. returned to Walt's original concept of a retirement home in which displaced spirits could spend their afterlives happily haunting any unsuspecting guests who came calling.

"The main reason for that was the sign that had been sitting out there for six years," Atencio explains. "We had been out gathering ghosts for all this time." And so in one final, ironic twist of fate, one of The Haunted Mansion's numerous delays had backed X.

into a makeshift story line. Marty Sklar's sign, inviting "all ghosts and restless spirits" to enjoy "active retirement" in these "happy haunting grounds" had presold Disneyland guests on the story. So that was what X. decided to give them.

Though not as intricately constructed as a Shakespearean play, a story exists. In fact, Imagineering legend and Disneyland veteran Tony Baxter believes that, in the end, combining the seemingly divergent work of Marc Davis and Claude Coats inadvertently gave The Haunted Mansion a fairly solid three-act structure. In Act One, which begins slowly and ominously in the Foyer, guests anticipate the appearance of the happy haunts, and experience poltergeist activity and unseen spirits. Madame Leota provides the curtain that separates Act One and Act Two. The medium conjures up the spirits and encourages them to materialize, which they promptly do in the swinging wake in the Grand Hall and the Attic. The descent from the attic window into the Graveyard takes guests into Act Three, in which they are completely surrounded by the ghosts who are enjoying the manic intensity of a graveyard jamboree. Finally, one of three Hitchhiking Ghosts materializes beside guests in their Doom Buggy before the exit. This might be a happy accident, as Imagineers refer to such serendipity, but it works.

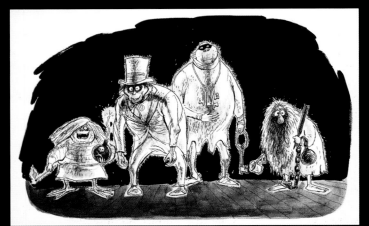

The Haunted Mansion's loose three-act structure can be seen in these concept renderings. The experience begins with a journey through ominous, character-free environments, such as this endless corridor (TOP LEFT), courtesy of Dorothea Redmond. In Marc Davis's concept sketches, Madame Leota's plaintive incantations cause the 999 happy haunts to materialize in Act Two (TOP RIGHT) for a "swinging wake" that begins in the Grand Hall (CENTER LEFT) and culminates in the Graveyard of Act Three (CENTER RIGHT) where restless spirits surround guests and (LEFT) ultimately follow them home.

THE END IS NIGH

As the 1960s drew to an end, The Haunted Mansion entered the home stretch after spending so many years in development. Marc and Claude married their characters and sets into finished show scenes. X. polished a show script that united stretching portrait chambers, endless corridors, a disembodied spirit in a crystal ball, a jilted bride pining for her long-lost

groom even in death, and a graveyard jamboree. Blaine Gibson and Wathel Rogers brought the happy haunts to life through the symbiotic arts of sculpture and Audio-Animatronics. And Yale Gracey put the finishing touches on special effects and illusions that had been more than ten years in the making.

Nearly a half decade after the old plantation house first appeared on a hill overlooking the Rivers of America, it welcomed its first human tenants in the Imagineers who readied the Mansion for the 999 grinning ghosts that would soon be taking up eternal residence at Disneyland. Out of sight and out of mind on the other side of the berm, a construction crew was erecting the mammoth show building that would house the attraction.

THE OPENING

As The Haunted Mansion's opening day drew closer, everyone at Disneyland and WED began to realize that the anticipation was even greater than they had imagined. Wild rumors and urban legends had been building for six years, ever since that notorious sign first appeared on the newly constructed Mansion's gate in 1963.

One of the more infamous rumors seemed appropriate for a haunted mansion, as X. Atencio told *Storyboard* magazine. "There was a rumor that a reporter had suffered a heart attack in there and we had to shut it down because it was too scary, and we had to change things. It was embellished over and over, so there might be a few versions of it. You have the first shakedown [a technical run-through that allows the designers to make adjustments], and that's probably where the reporter story

TOP, LEFT TO RIGHT: The Haunted Mansion shield evolves from sketch to reality. **LEFT:** Yale Gracey tests a friend's reflexes as the Mansion's opening day draws near.

started. You have a press opening and things still aren't working. It takes a while to get everything going, and I think we did have to shut it down for a while to work out some of the gags that weren't really coming off."

All the rumors and misinformation would only work to the Mansion's advantage. After eighteen years of on-again, off-again development and six years of anticipation created by the empty house on the hill, The Haunted Mansion's doors finally creaked open on August 9, 1969, and rewarded Disneyland for its patience when it set a single-day attendance record of 82,516 on August 16, exactly one week after opening. The attraction was an instant hit and has remained a Disneyland favorite for more than thirty years, a masterpiece of Imagineering that has been successfully adapted in three other Magic Kingdom Parks around the world.

RIGHT: An early concept rendering of the attraction poster that hangs in the tunnels beneath Disneyland Train Station. **BELOW:** The opening days of The Haunted Mansion, when an open house often meant closing the park due to record crowds.

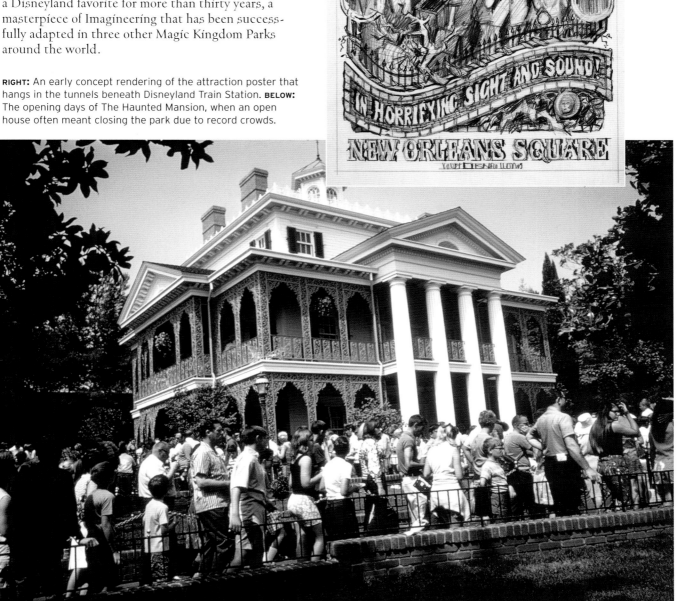

Two of a Kind: Walt Disney World and Tokyo Disneyland

PROJECT X

THE HAUNTED MANSION was an unqualifed success and sent Disneyland turnstiles spinning, but it would not remain unique to The Happiest Place on Earth for very long. By the time the attraction began to gain some momentum in 1967, earth already had begun to move in the swampland outside Orlando, Florida, for Walt Disney World (or Project X, as it was known within WED). The East Coast resort was slated to open in October 1971 and the decision was made early on to include The Haunted Mansion at Magic Kingdom Park at Walt Disney World.

Since the two attractions were scheduled to open within less than two years of each other, Imagineers decided to make two of everything from the start. The duplicate interiors were constructed simultaneously, with one set going straight to Disneyland and the other put into storage until the show building in Florida was ready to receive it. However, once again there was the question of where the building would land on the map.

A DIFFERENT WORLD

Imagineers knew they couldn't reproduce the exterior of the Disneyland Mansion at the Magic Kingdom because they had already eliminated the Southern-style New Orleans Square. But they also recognized that when Walt Disney World opened in 1971, America's Bicentennial would be just a few short years away. With that in mind, they pulled out Walt's old concept of Liberty Street and used it as the basis for a larger and more elaborate Liberty Square, the new home of a finally realized The Hall of Presidents and, it was decided, The Haunted Mansion.

Liberty Square, like the concept of Liberty Street before it, would re-create life in the original thirteen colonies. This geographical shift led Imagineers to New York's lower Hudson River Valley, the ancestral home of Sleepy Hollow and the Headless Horseman, and they were inspired by the region's stately old manor houses, in which English, Dutch, and German settlers would gather by the fireside and spin tales of the supernatural such as those by Washington Irving. Just as the Disneyland Mansion owed a debt to the Shipley-Lydecker House in Baltimore, the Walt Disney World version likely drew some of its inspiration from the very same catalog of Victorian-era design. It has also been claimed that Imagineers visited the Harry Packer Mansion, a Gothic manse built in 1874 in Jim Thorpe, Pennsylvania.

So The Haunted Mansion was transformed from an antebellum, Southern mansion into a Dutch Gothic–style manor house to fit in with its new Colonial surroundings. The final design incorporated a number of strong Gothic design elements typical of pre-Revolutionary New York's lower Hudson River Valley, including arches thrusting upward into the sky, large stone foundations and cornerstones, and the stone and brickwork common to the English Tudor style. This particular type of architecture is referred to as Perpendicular Style for its use of strong vertical lines, which enhance the sense that the Mansion is towering above you, tall and forbidding. The style was chosen precisely because Imagineers wanted the Mansion's exterior to look a bit scarier than the Disneyland original. To that end, Claude Coats himself played with the scale and some of the ornamentation to make the Mansion appear even more sinister and foreboding. The Mansion's two wings seem almost clawlike in appearance, as though the house is looming over you, ready to attack. Despite warning signs, the Disneyland Mansion's relatively benign appearance had led many parents to believe the attraction would be appropriate for all ages, only to discover the experience was too in-

tense for small children. Imagineers wanted to avoid that problem at the Magic Kingdom by dropping a much bigger hint as to what guests could expect before they entered the queue.

The entire attraction was installed and ready to go by April 1971, a full half year before the new park was scheduled to open. The decision to build the Florida Mansion right alongside its Disneyland sibling was a smart one, and The Haunted Mansion turned out to be one of the easiest projects in Walt Disney World history.

OPPOSITE: The Dutch Gothic–style Haunted Mansion at Walt Disney World. **TOP:** Walt Disney World attraction poster. **ABOVE:** The Haunted Mansion under construction. The gargantuan show building dwarfs the relatively small entry facade. **LEFT:** Herb Ryman's concept art of a pre-Revolutionary manor house straight out of New York's lower Hudson River Valley, a vastly different interpretation of The Haunted Mansion from the one that was built.

FRIGHTS OF FANTASY— TOKYO STYLE

When Imagineers began to develop ideas for Tokyo Disneyland, the first Disney-branded theme park outside the United States, they knew they would replicate many of the existing Magic Kingdom's signature rides and attractions, including The Haunted Mansion. Once again, their biggest challenge was where to put it. There would be no formal New Orleans Square (although elements of it were used to create Pirates of the Caribbean and its environs in Adventureland), nor a Liberty Square, which was considered a uniquely American experience. The Haunted Mansion was temporarily homeless, and Imagineers would have to find a place for it in one of the Magic Kingdom's other lands. Although the Mansion had been planned for both Main Street, U.S.A., and Frontierland at various times throughout its history, the attraction just didn't seem appropriate for the Tokyo park's version of those two lands, World Bazaar and Westernland. The search continued.

Imagineers ultimately found their answer in the Japanese culture itself, in which ghost stories are often categorized as fairy tales or fables. Since fairy tales belonged in the Magic Kingdom Fantasyland, so, then,

TOP LEFT: An illustration in the same book of Victorian-era design that contained a picture of the Shipley-Lydecker House likely inspired the Claude Coates–influenced rendering of the Haunted Mansion that is more sinister and foreboding than earlier concepts for the Florida attraction **(TOP CENTER). TOP RIGHT:** The griffinlike creatures at the Tokyo Disneyland Haunted Mansion help tie the attraction into its Fantasyland location.

ABOVE AND RIGHT: Imagineers prepare The Haunted Mansion for its first trip outside the United States to Japan. **OPPOSITE TOP:** Tokyo attraction poster. **OPPOSITE BOTTOM:** With its early American architecture and fanciful subject matter, The Haunted Mansion provides a seamless transition between Fantasyland and Frontierland (later Critter Country) at Tokyo Disneyland.

would The Haunted Mansion. Now the attraction had a home, but what would it look like? The Tokyo park's Fantasyland, like its sibling in Florida, was to have a distinct European influence that began with the French Gothic Cinderella Castle. The Haunted Mansion at Walt Disney World also had a European flavor thanks to the taste in architecture the early English and Dutch settlers brought with them to the New World. The Florida Mansion had always looked perfectly natural when viewed from the banks of the Rivers of America in Frontierland, so Imagineers decided the same design would help them build a nice thematic bridge between Fantasyland and Westernland in the new park. And so The Haunted Mansion was destined to go Dutch Gothic once again at Tokyo Disneyland.

The Tokyo Disneyland Mansion is a direct lift of the Walt Disney World version; the two are virtually identical inside and out. Imagineers made only one key addition to the exterior by adding two large, faux bronze griffinlike creatures that sit atop the columns of the Mansion's front gate. The appearance of these decidedly fantastic creatures further helped the Mansion fit in with its Fantasyland surroundings while remaining true to its Gothic style.

Less than ten years after the opening of Tokyo Disneyland, The Haunted Mansion would find itself on the move once again, and this time Imagineers would build the attraction's future on a foundation that had been laid in the distant past.

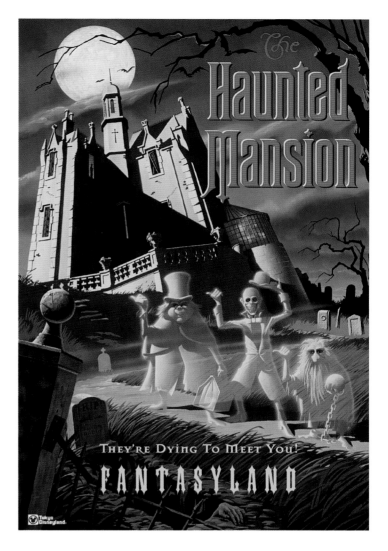

Grim Grinning Ghosts Go West

A FRENCH TWIST

I N 1984, plans were set in motion to build Disneyland Paris, a Walt Disney World–style theme park and resort destination located in Marne-la-Vallée, a verdant agricultural region twenty miles east of Paris, France. The centerpiece of the resort would be a new interpretation of Disney's flagship theme park in Anaheim. Imagineer and Disneyland veteran Tony Baxter was assigned to lead the creative team that would reinvent the Magic Kingdom experience for a European audience. Unlike their Japanese counterparts, French officials weren't interested in a wholesale reproduction of Disney's American parks, which meant that Imagineers would have to translate their stories to appeal to a very different culture. This reinvention enabled Imagineers to revisit some of their own signature attractions, and in the case of The Haunted Mansion, that meant coming full circle.

YOU CAN GO HOME AGAIN

The Haunted Mansion finally came "home" to Frontierland, decades after Ken Anderson's first story concepts, more by default than anything else. There would be no New Orleans Square or Liberty Square at the new park, and Main Street, U.S.A., was already crowded with buildings. A Fantasyland Haunted Mansion didn't make the same cultural sense as it did in Japan. After ruling out Adventureland and

OPPOSITE: Concept art by Dan Goozee ultimately used in the attraction poster for Phantom Manor at Disneyland Paris. TOP AND ABOVE: Imagineers Tony Baxter and Jeff Burke moved The Haunted Mansion "back" to Frontierland. BELOW: A concept painting of Frontierland by Tom Gilleon.

Discovery land (the Disneyland Paris version of Tomorrowland) for obvious reasons, the only logical place for The Haunted Mansion was Frontierland.

A Frontierland setting in France turned out to be just as culturally appropriate as the Fantasyland location in Japan. "Gothic mansions and graveyards are part of the neighborhood in France—they see them every day. There's nothing exotic or magical about it," says Tony Baxter. "We had to do something that would be appealing to that audience."

One thing the French audience did have in common with the Japanese was a fascination with the fabled American Wild West. The dastardly outlaws, heroic cowboys and Indians, and panoramic vistas of the fruited plains carried a distinction unseen in Europe.

Frontierland would become a particularly strong component of the new park. Tony Baxter and executive designer Jeff Burke fashioned an elaborate back story to serve as a foundation for all of Frontierland that combined the story lines of Phantom Manor and the classic attraction Big Thunder Mountain Railroad with the newly created wild and woolly Gold Rush town of Thunder Mesa.

THUNDER MESA

Thunder Mesa and its outlying regions were inspired by characters and settings originally created for "Western River Expedition," a Wild West version of Pirates of the Caribbean that Marc Davis had once developed for the Walt Disney World Magic Kingdom. In Tony and Jeff's new story, the centerpiece of Thunder Mesa was Big Thunder Mountain, which occupies an island in the middle of the Rivers of the Far West (standing in for Tom Sawyer Island and Rivers of America, respectively). According to legend, there was gold in

that thar mountain, and industrial baron Henry Ravens-wood set up the Thunder Mesa Mining Company to help "lighten the lode." Ravenswood struck it rich, and a boomtown sprung up around his mining operation, creating the dusty streets and sunbaked wooden buildings of Frontierland in the process. The story's craggy mountain range and the labyrinthine gold mine within set the stage for the runaway trains of Big Thunder Mountain Railroad; and, as fate would have it, Henry Ravenswood would also provide a home for Phantom Manor . . . literally.

THE LEGEND OF PHANTOM MANOR

Flush with his earnings from the mine at the height of the Gold Rush, Henry Ravenswood built a stately Victorian manor high atop a hill overlooking the town of Thunder Mesa and the mine that built it. Nothing was too good for his wife, Martha, and their young daughter, Melanie. But the gold eventually ran out, and Henry Ravenswood's luck along with it. Then a great earthquake struck Thunder Mesa in 1860, during preparations for Melanie Ravenswood's wedding.

Henry and Martha perished in the quake, and their daughter was never seen again . . . or was she? Their once magnificent home fell into a state of disrepair and neglect. Eerie shadows could sometimes be seen through the dingy windows and strange sounds came from within, leading locals to dub the old house the "Phantom Manor." But what really happened on the day of the earthquake? Was Melanie Ravenswood alive or dead? And what happened to her groom?

The Manor's true story was revealed long after the deaths of Henry and Martha Ravenswood and the disappearance of their daughter. Melanie's fiancé had planned to move her far away from Thunder Mesa . . . and her father. Henry Ravenswood disapproved and vowed to stop the wedding at all costs, but that fateful earthquake prevented him from doing so . . . or did it? Locals believe that the mysterious Phantom is actually Henry Ravenswood himself, who murdered his daughter's intended from beyond the grave to keep her from marrying against his wishes. Melanie survived but never left the house, wandering through the Manor in her bridal gown until her dying day and beyond. Henry Ravenswood never left, either—dead set on keeping his daughter in Thunder Mesa forever. Melanie's intended still hangs around as well—in the stretching chamber, by a rope around his neck, that is.

Now the domestic staff has finally opened up the house to tell their story and allow visitors to try to unlock the secrets of the Manor for themselves. Guests quickly discover that the Phantom and the Bride-never-to-be are engaged in an eternal struggle for Ravenswood Manor and the souls of everyone who dares enter. The Phantom and his army of ghosts, ghouls, and goblins make every attempt to lure unsuspecting visitors to the other side, while the Bride struggles to help her mortal friends live to tell the secret of Phantom Manor.

OPPOSITE TOP: A painting of Ravenswood Manor during its glory days . . . but even then dark clouds hung over the old house on the hill. **OPPOSITE BOTTOM:** The history of Thunder Mesa as depicted in this overall view by John Horny. **THIS PAGE:** In Phantom Manor, the struggle between good and evil is personified by the benevolent bride, Melanie Ravenswood (**TOP**), and the vile Phantom (**ABOVE**), who just may be her father, Henry. **LEFT:** Concept art of Phantom Manor by Dan Goozee.

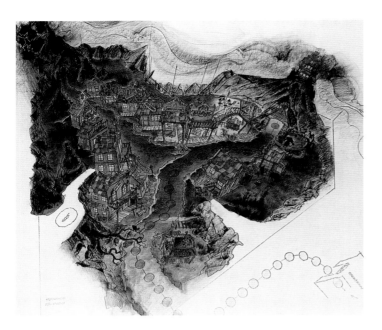

THE HOUSE ON THE HILL

Phantom Manor is perhaps the most sinister-looking of all the Haunted Mansions thanks to its gloomy, ramshackle appearance, which appears to go against Walt's desire for a pristine exterior. The design of the house, like the attraction's name change, was driven by the need to translate the experience for guests from all over Europe. Imagineers needed to visually convey as much story content as possible, relying less on the spoken word. Phantom Manor's exterior had to clearly communicate what guests could expect inside.

Most of downtown Frontierland looks like it came straight out of the archetypal Old West of Tombstone, Arizona, but the wealthy part of town in which Phantom Manor is located was inspired by 19th-century Virginia City, Nevada. In fact, the Manor bears a striking resemblance to that city's Fourth Ward Schoolhouse, a four-story Victorian structure still standing today, as well as the Addams Family–like mansion seen in that first Harper Goff sketch from 1951.

SOUNDS SCARY

The original Mansion's look wasn't the only show element to undergo "a disquieting metamorphosis." The attraction's signature music also received a full makeover. Film composer John Debney (*I Know What You Did Last Summer; Bruce Almighty*) took Buddy Baker and X. Atencio's original composition of "Grim Grinning Ghosts" and added lush orchestral arrangements, which underscore the attraction much like a film sound track. The classic piece is also heard as an eerie, music box tune and a honky-tonk piano version played in a ghostly saloon. Imagineer and amateur opera singer Katherine Meyering even provided the Bride's lilting soprano for a mournful, solo rendition of the song. The music was performed by the London Chamber Orchestra at the city's famous Abbey Road Studios.

Like its predecessors, Phantom Manor features memorable vocal performances. When Imagineers put together a temporary sound track for the attraction, they used Vincent Price's trademark cackle from the end of Michael Jackson's pop classic *Thriller* to create the Phantom's evil laugh. From that moment on, Vincent Price was the Phantom as far as they were concerned, and he was brought in to record a new interpretation of the Ghost Host's narration for the Foyer, Stretch Room, and Portrait Corridor scenes.

The horror film legend's run was short-lived, as fate would have it. Shortly after the attraction opened, operators requested a French version of the narration. The Ghost Host's minimal dialogue was re-recorded by French actor Gérard Chevalier although Vincent Price's performance of the Phantom's infamous laugh can still be heard throughout the attraction.

TOP: A ghostly vision of Thunder Mesa can be seen far below Phantom Manor in this concept design. **BELOW LEFT:** The Fourth Ward Schoolhouse in Virginia City, Nevada. **BELOW RIGHT:** An Imagineer adjusts the model of Phantom Manor.

Oona Lind took over as Madame Leota, reciting her incantations in both French and English. Oona also provides the crowd-pleasing "Hurry back" dialogue at the end of the attraction, this time delivered by the Bride herself, not "Little Leota." And the original Ghost Host makes a cameo appearance as the mayor of a ghostly version of Thunder Mesa, which replaces the Graveyard scene as the attraction's climax.

Phantom Manor opened with the rest of Disneyland Paris on April 12, 1992, and quickly became one of the park's most popular attractions and something of a cult classic with Disney and Haunted Mansion fans all over the world. It may be the most recent incarnation of The Haunted Mansion, though Imagineers and guests alike wouldn't bet on its being the last.

TOP LEFT: Master of horror Vincent Price records lines for the new Ghost Host as (**LEFT TO RIGHT**) Ken Lisi, audio project management; Greg Meader, audio production; and Gabrielle Reynolds, casting director, look on. **TOP RIGHT:** A rendering of Melanie Ravenswood's doomed wedding party, a concept dating back to some of Ken Anderson's original story lines. **ABOVE:** The mayor of Thunder Mesa, voiced by the original Ghost Host, Paul Frees, seen here tipping his hat (his head will soon follow) to passing guests. **LEFT:** Phantom Manor. The name was chosen because it means roughly the same thing in English and French.

Second Story

A Tour of Wall-to-Wall Creeps

THE GROUNDS

"When hinges creak in doorless chambers and strange and frightening sounds echo through the halls . . ."

GUESTS PASS THROUGH The Haunted Mansion's ornate entrance gates to find themselves on its meticulously landscaped grounds. Originally, a collection of tombstones made up a "family plot," X. Atencio's macabre salute to the Imagineers who built the mansion. Guests were able to pay their respects and read the frightfully funny epitaphs before the queue was eventually enlarged and the headstones removed. (X. took his own tablet and moved it into his backyard.)

PRECEDING SPREAD: Night lights at the Disneyland Haunted Mansion. **ABOVE:** In the ultimate tribute, the legendary Imagineers who worked on The Haunted Mansion were immortalized—literally—by X. Atencio in the humorous epitaphs he wrote for the tombstones in the family plot outside the Mansion.

ENHANCEMENTS
Pet Cemetery

What many guests thought was an urban legend is actually true—there was, indeed, a pet cemetery hidden in an enclosed garden at the side of the Disneyland Haunted Mansion. The original was located on the right side, near what is now Splash Mountain. It was created in the early 1980s by Imagineering's senior concept designer for Disneyland, Kim Irvine—the daughter of Madame Leota

herself, Leota Toombs—who bought pieces of statuary from local nurseries and turned to show writer Chris Goosman to compose humorous epitaphs for the lost pets. This hidden gem proved to be such a hit that Imagineers made it official,

creating a permanent pet cemetery along the attraction's queue in 1993. Pet cemeteries have since been added to all the other incarnations of The Haunted Mansion.

Hearse to You

In the early 1990s, Imagineer Bob Baranick convinced Disneyland to purchase a hearse from a local antiques dealer for use in a proposed Young Indiana Jones Epic Stunt Spectacular. When plans for the show were eliminated, Bob proposed placing the hearse outside The Haunted Mansion, but Tony Baxter, Disneyland's creative lead at the time, countered that a hearse sitting by itself didn't make enough story sense. Inspired by the wildly popular "invisible dogs on a leash" that were sold at the park, Tony proposed hitching the hearse to a phantom horse. This appropriate photo op made its debut in September 1995 and proved to be such a hit that a similar enhancement was quickly added to Walt Disney World.

Contrary to another stubborn urban legend, the white Disneyland hearse was not used to transport Brigham Young to his final resting place. However, the black hearse at Walt Disney World did have its own "brush with greatness"—it was used in the 1965 John Wayne film The Sons of Katie Elder.

A closer look at the Florida and Tokyo Mansion's exteriors yields some interesting design details. The weather vane atop the cupola is a bat, replacing the Disneyland original's sailing ship. It is an ironic design change, considering that many such manor houses throughout the Hudson River Valley and New England actually did have sailing ships for weather vanes. A piece of foreshadowing is the dead wreath hanging on the front door, and tombstones still provide macabre merriment before entering the attraction. The small glass-and-steel structure attached to the side of the Mansion is a view of the conservatory from the outside, although there is no hint of the premature funeral taking place inside.

Game Over

Over the years, many fans have speculated that the Mansion's stone turrets are oversized chess pieces, with every piece represented except the knight (who can be found inside, the urban legend says). Not so, according to Imagineers. Although some of the turrets and ornamentation do, indeed, look like chess pieces, all are typical of the Mansion's architectural style and period, and the resemblance is purely coincidental.

WALT DISNEY WORLD
Rest in Peace, Madame Leota

In 2001, a team of Imagineers, including senior vice president, creative development Eric Jacobson; design director Patrick Brennan; animator Doug Griffith; and yours truly, Jason Surrell, as their show writer, began looking for ways to use small-scale animation to enhance the guest experience throughout the park, especially in queues and areas where there was less to see and do. One result, which debuted in 2002, was a new tombstone in the far right corner of the family plot that sits outside the Mansion's entrance doors.

The headstone, which bears the sculpted face of a beautiful young woman, reads:

> DEAR SWEET LEOTA, BELOVED BY ALL,
> IN REGIONS BEYOND NOW, BUT HAVING A BALL

Not entirely resting at peace, the sculpture frequently opens her eyes slowly, watching guests as they proceed through the portico, and then closes her eyes, returning once more to her eternal sleep. This subtle but spooky welcome sets an appropriately ominous tone as guests begin their tour. They shake their head and enter the Mansion, asking themselves: "Did that really move or am I seeing things?"

This will not be guests' last encounter with Madame Leota. Her tombstone, combined with the character's appearance in Séance Circle, creates a bit more structure for the overall story. Perhaps even more important than its story value, the tombstone finally enables Leota Toombs to take her rightful place alongside her fellow Mansion Imagineers.

ABOVE LEFT: The tombstone honoring Claude Coats.
ABOVE RIGHT: Cast Members often cut a fresh red rose from the garden and place it atop Yale Gracey's headstone in a silent homage to the "master" of special effects.

Master Class

"Master Gracey's" tombstone was X.'s tribute to special-effects wizard Yale Gracey and has led many fans to incorrectly assume that the master of the house—and thus the Ghost Host—is named Gracey. This urban legend took on such a life of its own over the years that it has become an accepted part of Haunted Mansion lore almost by default. In fact, when it came time to name "The Master" in *The Haunted Mansion* movie, filmmakers named him Gracey in honor of Yale and the rumors spawned by his tombstone.

 Although the layout of Phantom Manor is quite similar to that of the other Haunted Mansions, the more elaborate story line and detailed characterizations prompted the creation of some major new scenes as well as additions and enhancements to existing favorites.

As guests make their way up an old carriage road, they stroll across the manor's desolate grounds and pass a rickety old gazebo and a crumbling garden pavilion that complement the house's run-down, decaying appearance. Eerie flickering lights and the shadow of the mysterious Bride can be seen in the house's dingy windows.

ENHANCEMENTS
Disneyland Haunted Mansion Holiday

In the late 1990s, inspired by the success of their seasonal enhancement, It's A Small World Holiday, Disneyland officials began looking for other attractions to decorate for the holidays. "In 1997 we created a holiday overlay for It's A Small World that was a major hit," creative entertainment director Steve Davison recalls. "We found that guests liked the idea of seeing an attraction enhanced. They relive their old memories of the ride while making new ones created from the holiday version. Plus, guests treat these classic rides with ownership—they want to come and see what you have done to 'their' ride. Disneyland has that effect on people."

Imagineers proposed a retelling of Charles Dickens's A Christmas Carol, set inside The Haunted Mansion but the park declined. Then Creative Entertainment suggested retelling 'Twas the Night Before Christmas. Instead of introducing Santa Claus into such a macabre environment, Imagineering suggested instead using Tim Burton's The Nightmare Before Christmas. The concept was put into development with Davison at the helm and the result, Haunted Mansion Holiday, was Disneyland's early Christmas gift to the world when it premiered in October 2001.

"We consulted Tim Burton on all the designs," Steve says. "The director and designers of the film, who were there opening day, were thrilled to see some of their early concepts like the 'Countdown to Christmas' clock now in human scale with every detail that was in the film."

In the story line's merrily macabre makeover, the 999 happy haunts invite Jack Skellington, dressed in his signature "Sandy Claws" suit, to deck their halls for the Yuletide season. Madame Leota offers a spooky new holiday greeting in Séance Circle, the Grand Hall is the scene of the ultimate Christmas party, and the Graveyard is blanketed in ghostly white snow, with playful spooks busy making their own unique Christmas trees. As guests leave the Mansion, Jack's longtime love, Sally, stands in for Little Leota, urging guests to return and spend the holidays with 999 of their closest, ghostly friends.

The holiday-themed show called for new footage of Madame Leota, though the role's originator, Leota Toombs, had passed away years earlier. In a fortunate twist of fate, Leota's daughter, Kim Irvine, works at Disneyland as an Imagineer and bears a startling resemblance to her mother. So Kim performed Madame Leota's eerie incantations as her mother had done more than thirty years earlier. Now mother and daughter are forever united, working together to create the magic of Madame Leota.

THE FOYER

"Whenever candle lights flicker . . . where the air is deathly still . . . that is the time when ghosts are present, practicing their terror with ghoulish delight."

ABOVE: A concept rendering of the marble bust that the Ghost Host was to "possess" in the foyer of the Disneyland Haunted Mansion.

THE GHOST HOST, the unseen presence that escorts guests through the Mansion, begins his infamous narration in the Foyer, underscored by "Grim Grinning Ghosts" arranged as an ominous funeral dirge. Veteran character actor and master voice-over artist Paul Frees was cast as the voice and has become such a beloved part of the experience that many guests deliver the dialogue right along with him. Among his other credits, Frees provided voices for Boris Badenov on *The Adventures of Rocky and Bullwinkle*, Disney's own Ludwig Von Drake, and numerous other Disney attraction characters.

Imagineers originally planned for the Ghost Host's opening narration to be delivered "live" by a marble bust that suddenly came to life, but they found that guests were preoccupied talking among themselves and either too excited or too nervous about what they were going to see to really pay attention. The Ghost Host's brief but effective verbal set-up proved to be more than enough activity for the small space. At the conclusion of his opening monologue, a panel in the Foyer wall slides open to reveal one of two identical Portrait Chambers.

TOP, PAGES 54-55: The master of the house ages, Dorian Gray–style, before guests' eyes in a portrait hanging in the foyer of the Walt Disney World and Tokyo Disneyland Haunted Mansions. **LEFT:** Paul Frees

 Although there are no show elements in The Haunted Mansion's Foyer at Disneyland other than the Ghost Host's narration, Imagineers decided to add a visual effect to the Florida and Tokyo Mansions, given the opportunity. As guests enter the Foyer, their attention is drawn to a formal portrait of the master of the house hanging on the wall above the fireplace. Contrary to another popular theory that has made the rounds over the years, the Ghost Host is *not* the master of the house—Gracey or otherwise—but merely one of 999 happy haunts. As the Ghost Host delivers his infamous narration, the image in the portrait transforms, Dorian Gray–style, from that of a handsome young man to that of a rotting corpse. It is a chilling premonition of the Ghost Host's fate, which guests are about to see firsthand in the Portrait Chamber.

As will be seen in the transforming pictures in the Portrait Corridor in Disneyland, this illusion is created by a digital effect that replaced a series of overlapping still images during a 2007 enhancement. The Foyer is the only room in the Walt Disney World and Tokyo Disneyland versions of the attraction to feature a transforming portrait effect.

 Unlike its siblings in America and Japan, the Phantom Manor story begins immediately as guests enter the Foyer. A faint image of the ill-fated Bride appears in an ornate mirror as the Ghost Host begins to tell her tale of lost love.

LEFT: Servants (the direct descendants of Beauregard the Butler from early story treatments) greet guests and usher them into the Foyer, seen here in costume design sketches created for Tokyo Disneyland. **ABOVE:** The ghostly image of Melanie Ravenswood appears in a mirror in the Phantom Manor's Foyer, an effect designed to begin the story as soon as guests step inside the house.

PORTRAIT CHAMBER
(The Stretching Room)

"Our tour begins here, in this gallery. . . ."

ABOVE: A concept rendering of the Portrait Chamber prior to its "disquieting metamorphosis." **LEFT:** The Portrait Chamber's fan-favorite gargoyle sconce. **OPPOSITE TOP:** Marc Davis concept renderings of the legendary stretching portraits, including, according to a 1968 X. Atencio script, "Alexander Nitrokoff...an anarchist who came to us with a bang one night" **(CENTER LEFT)** and "Widow Abigale Patecleaver, who was preceded by her husband," the ill-fated George **(CENTER RIGHT). OPPOSITE BOTTOM:** The Portrait Chamber at Walt Disney World.

IN THE PORTRAIT CHAMBER, guests see "paintings of some of our guests as they appeared in their corruptible, mortal state," which are all Marc Davis originals. Once guests drag their bodies into the dead center of the room, the panel slides shut, sealing them into an octagonal space complete with grinning gargoyles holding flickering candles. We are reminded that the chamber "has no windows and no doors." Without warning, the entire room begins to "stretch," and the portraits elongate to reveal the comically creepy fates of their subjects. The Ghost Host then offers guests a chilling challenge—to find a way out.

"Of course, there's always my way," he concludes as lightning flashes to reveal a corpse dangling from a hangman's noose in the cupola high above. The lights wink out, and a shrill scream fills the air.

At the scene's conclusion, a panel in the wall of each of the two Portrait Chambers slides open to reveal one long, dimly lit corridor.

THE SCENE IS A NOD to Ken Anderson's Captain Gore story, in which the captain hanged himself in the attic after murdering his young bride. The room that stretches was a creative solution to an operational problem. In order to meet the park's capacity requirements, the attraction was housed in an enormous show building outside Disneyland's berm. Imagineers needed to move them below ground to the show building "outside" the park. So, in the Stretching Room, the ceiling remains in place while the floor lowers, taking guests fifteen feet underground to a corridor that transports them under the railroad tracks into the show building itself.

The four "stretching" portraits unfurl to reach their full dimensions, extending from three to eight feet, as the elevator makes its descent.

The ceiling is a theatrical scrim, a piece of fabric that is opaque when lit from the front (and painted to look like the chamber's ceiling) and translucent when lit from behind, in this case by "lightning," revealing the decaying corpse of the Ghost Host hanging from previously unseen rafters.

The grim fate of the Ghost Host himself, seen here in a series of concept sketches and a rare, eye-socket level view of the finished figure.

THE PORTRAIT CHAMBER

When Imagineers originally designed The Haunted Mansion for Disneyland, they had to deal with some serious spatial constraints due to the Park's relatively small size. That was not the case with Walt Disney World and Tokyo Disneyland, so their version of The Haunted Mansion contains some enhancements and scenes that aren't found in the original.

As there was no longer a need to move guests down to and away from the show building for the attraction, since the attraction was safely ensconced inside each park, the necessity for the unique Stretching Room was eliminated. However, since the Portrait Chamber had become such a beloved part of the show, the scene was left in place. The effect is exactly the same as in the California version, but instead of the floor *lowering*, the ceiling *rises*, and guests move directly into the load area on the same floor level.

As part of the 2007 enhancement to the Walt Disney World Haunted Mansion, Imagineers implemented a state-of-the-art three-dimensional audio system for the Portrait Chamber to create the illusion that the Ghost Host is gliding around the room as he delivers his infamous narration. When the room begins to stretch, a low rumbling emanates from the floor, and the walls begin to moan and groan as guests actually *hear* and *feel* the chamber elongating around them for the first time. Once the Ghost Host's grim fate is revealed and the lights go out, guests hear the disquieting fluttering of bats' wings accompanying the familiar descending scream—as though the supernatural commotion has disturbed their peaceful slumber. If guests listen closely as they file out of the Portrait Chamber, they can actually hear playful voices urging them to "stay together" and, ultimately, "get out!"

ABOVE: Neil Engel sketch that captured the decidedly special effect that the addition of three-dimensional audio effects would have on the Portrait Chamber in the 2007 Walt Disney World enhancement. **RIGHT, TOP AND BOTTOM:** The stretching portraits in Phantom Manor depict four different but equally grim fates of Melanie Ravenswood, the first indication that things are going to end badly for the young bride.

THE SECRET ROOM

At Phantom Manor, Julie Svendsen's striking paintings of a young Melanie Ravenswood replace Marc Davis's quirky portraits. As the room begins to stretch, the portraits elongate to reveal the gleefully grim fate awaiting the Bride in each one. When the lights go out, the lightning flashes to reveal the Phantom hanging his daughter's intended from the rafters high above, setting the story's central conflict into motion.

As in the Disneyland original, this portrait chamber, now dubbed "The Secret Room," serves as an elevator that transports guests underground, where they travel through a corridor that takes them underneath a tree-dotted hillside into the show building beyond.

THE PORTRAIT CORRIDOR

"There are several prominent ghosts who have retired here from creepy old crypts all over the world."

ACH GROUP OF GUESTS empties into the Portrait Corridor, one after the other, creating a virtually endless stream of people flowing toward the Load Area.

The left side of the corridor is lined with windows that overlook a moonlit landscape, intermittently illuminated by violent flashes of lightning. Portraits hang on the wall to the right, the subject of each slowly transforming into a nightmarish image as the viewer gazes upon it. At the far end of the hallway, two ominous-looking marble busts sit in recesses within the wall. As guests proceed down the corridor, they come face-to-face with the busts, one of which appears to be that of a Roman Emperor, and the other a rather stern-looking woman resembling an old schoolmarm. Both busts appear to follow the guests' every move—up, down, backward, and forward—as they make their way past them and into the adjacent Load Area.

THE MOVING BUST ILLUSION was one of Rolly Crump's so-called happy accidents. As part of their research and development for The Hall of Presidents, the Imagineers had created a mold of Abraham Lincoln's face, an artificial life mask of sorts. One day, Rolly and Yale happened to stroll past the backside of the face, and, as they did so, realized that from the reverse angle it appeared as though Honest Abe's eyes were following their every move. When lit from behind, the busts appear to be completely three-dimensional, facing out into the corridor.

The transforming portrait illusion depicts each subject in various stages of transformation. The images overlap, slowly and perfectly, gradually transforming the original subject into an eerie doppelganger. Most, if not all, of the portraits are based on Marc Davis concepts—another showcase for his decidedly lighter approach to The Haunted Mansion's macabre material. In a January 2005 enhancement to the Disneyland attraction, the Imagineers updated the transforming portraits with new technology that enabled them to realize the original design team's creative vision of images that would change in perfect time with the lightning flashes outside.

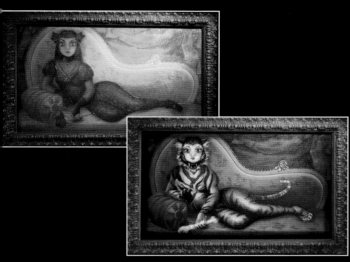

TOP: The Portrait Corridor in concept art for the Disneyland original (LEFT) and the 2007 Walt Disney World enhancement (RIGHT). CENTER LEFT: A transforming portrait as it appeared after a 2005 enhancement at Disneyland. CENTER RIGHT: A Marc Davis rendering of a portrait that never made it into the show.

LEFT AND ABOVE: Two views of Disneyland's Portrait Corridor show the portraits before and after.

After boarding a Doom Buggy, guests proceed down a long corridor, the right wall of which is lined with portraits.

During the 2007 enhancement of the Walt Disney World attraction, the original paintings with "moving eyes" in the Portrait Corridor were replaced with four of the new and improved transforming portraits from Disneyland. Synchronized with lightning flashes through large windows to the left, the portraits undergo startling transformations—the beautiful Medusa turns into a hideous Gorgon; a proud galleon devolves into a ghost ship; a gallant knight and his steed both become skeletons; and a beautiful young woman reclining on a couch is transformed into a white tiger.

Several of the displaced "moving eyes" portraits were relocated to the load area and along the staircase before the new Portrait Corridor.

RIGHT: This portrait of a vampire, ultimately used in Walt Disney World's Portrait Corridor, is based on an unused Marc Davis concept for a transforming portrait at Disneyland.
BELOW: The portrait of Melanie Ravenswood found in Phantom Manor's Portrait Gallery. BELOW RIGHT: Marc Davis concept art for a transforming portrait.

THE PORTRAIT GALLERY

The long hallway off the Secret Room houses a Portrait Gallery that features a number of transforming paintings, many based on original Marc Davis designs. At the very end of the gallery hangs a full-length portrait of the Bride, establishing her as a constant presence in the house and reinforcing her importance to the story.

THE LOAD AREA

"Do not pull down on the safety bar, please. I will lower it for you."

GUESTS PROCEED into a "limbo of boundless mist and decay," at least according to *The Story and Song from The Haunted Mansion*, a record album released in 1969. Guests step onto a moving walkway and climb into their Doom Buggy, where the Ghost Host is waiting to escort them on their tour of these happy haunting grounds.

TOP LEFT: An endless line of Doom Buggies stand ready to carry guests into the "moldering sanctum of the spirit world." **CENTER LEFT:** A cardboard Doom Buggy carries cardboard guests out of the Load Area in this scale model, complete with bat stanchion. **LEFT:** A Claude Coats rendering of a "limbo of boundless mist and decay," as described on *The Story and Song from The Haunted Mansion* record album (**ABOVE**).

In a small departure from the original Load Area, Florida and Tokyo Doom Buggies first move guests underneath a landing where a candelabra floats in inky blackness before descending into the inner sanctums of The Haunted Mansion.

The sculpted bats that top the stanchions in the Load Area are original designs, another testament to the Imagineers' commitment to detail. There are three styles of bats—two-winged, right-winged, and left-winged—to accommodate the various turns in the queue. But designers didn't just cut off a wing when they needed a bat with a single appendage—they entirely re-sculpted the piece. The other wing, fully styled, is folded at the bat's side.

The last bat that guests pass before boarding their Doom Buggies has been touched by literally millions of guests from around the world since opening day. If and when the bats are replaced, Imagineers may decide to leave it in place as a piece of living history.

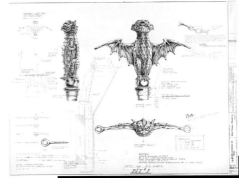

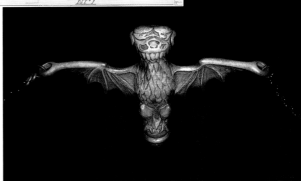

LEFT AND BELOW: A design drawing for the bat stanchion reveals the Imagineers' penchant for detail.

ABOVE: Concept art of the Grand Staircase in Phantom Manor's Load Area. RIGHT: The Grand Staircase as it appears in the attraction.

THE GRAND STAIRCASE

The Phantom Manor Load Area is a full show scene depicting a grand entry staircase. An enormous picture window at the top of the staircase looks onto a sinister, moonlit landscape illuminated by flashes of lightning. As the lightning flashes, the scene is drained of all color, becoming a melancholy, monochromatic gray landscape.

THE LIBRARY AND MUSIC ROOM

"Our library is well stocked with priceless first editions—only ghost stories, of course—and marble busts of the greatest ghost writers the literary world has ever known."

New Editions

 The Portrait Corridors at Walt Disney World and Tokyo Disneyland open into the Library, which is filled from floor to ceiling by shelves lined with hundreds of books. Phantom hands pull books from the shelves. A chair rocks gently back and forth, and a ladder slides to and fro as an unseen force searches for a good read. And among the shelves, those ubiquitous marble busts glare at guests as the Doom Buggies move past them in the gloom.

ALTHOUGH IT IS VIRTUALLY IMPOSSIBLE to see under the scene's eerie lighting, most of the Library set is a very convincing mural. The rocking chair, table, lamp, marble busts, and a few of the books are three-dimensional, but everything else is created through the use of "character paint," as Imagineers refer to it. The moving busts work in the exact same way as those in the Portrait Corridor at Disneyland.

The Music Room

A Rachmaninoff-style arrangement of "Grim Grinning Ghosts" fills the air as the Doom Buggies carry guests from the Library into a shadowy Music Room. A dust-covered square piano sits in the center of the room, playing by itself. Or so it seems. Bright moonlight streams through the Music Room window, casting a shadow of the pianist—actually the Ghost Host—onto the floor as he pounds away on the piano. The Doom Buggies then travel up a grand staircase past a few phosphorescent spiders to the Endless Hallway, where this version of The Haunted Mansion becomes nearly identical to the Disneyland original.

THE PIANO IS DRESSED UP to fit in with its ghostly surroundings. The Ghost Host's moving silhouette is a projection effect. A similar illusion was added to the Attic scene in Disneyland in the 1990s, with the unseen musician playing "The Wedding March."

LEFT: Disneyland's infamous moving busts—and two new ones—found a home in the Library at Walt Disney World and Tokyo Disneyland. **ABOVE:** "Moonlight" will cast the shadow of a ghostly pianist onto the floor of the Music Room.

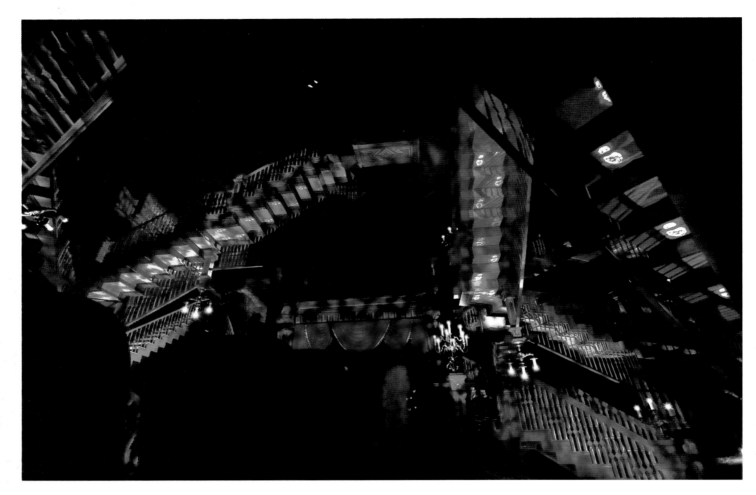

THE ENDLESS STAIRCASE

"We have 999 happy haunts here . . . but there's room for a thousand. Any volunteers?"

IN WALT DISNEY WORLD, a ghastly gargoyle crouched on the banister of the Grand Staircase leers down at the guests as they depart the music room. The Doom Buggies then ascend a nightmarish Endless Staircase. To the left and right of the main staircase, additional flights of stairs float illogically—in mid-air, right side up, and upside down—leading to and from nowhere, illuminated only by flickering candelabra. Even more disquieting, glowing green footsteps can be seen padding up and down the stairs! The unseen spirits blow out the candles in the candelabra, which then mysteriously re-light themselves.

Guests then proceed down a short, gloomy corridor in which glowing, bestial eyes stare at them from the darkness. The eyes blink and study the guests as the Doom Buggies pass by, revealing themselves to be coming from behind the wallpaper.

The 2007 enhancement in Walt Disney World finally gave the Imagineers an opportunity to realize a long-standing dream: that of replacing the former Grand Staircase's pitch blackness and two less-than-convincing rubber spiders with a more compelling show scene. The design team, led by portfolio leader Eric Jacobson and consisting of show producer Kathy Rogers, production designer Neil Engel, show writer Jason Surrell and principal media designer Joe Herrington among many others, considered everything from animated statues to digitally projected "virtual rooms" before settling on an "Endless Staircase." Creative executive Tom Fitzgerald felt strongly that the new scene should be "architectural" in nature, and staircases running every which way were partly inspired by some of Ken Anderson's original concept sketches as well as by one of his primary design influences, the Winchester Mystery House.

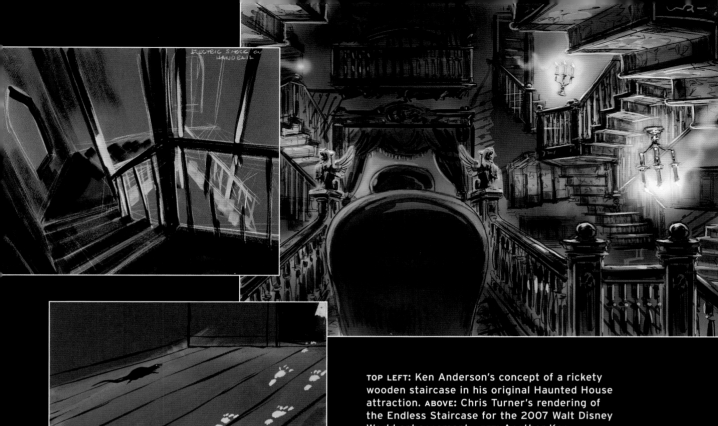

ELECTRIC SHOCK ON HANDRAIL

TOP LEFT: Ken Anderson's concept of a rickety wooden staircase in his original Haunted House attraction. **ABOVE:** Chris Turner's rendering of the Endless Staircase for the 2007 Walt Disney World enhancement. **LEFT:** Another Ken Anderson concept, this one depicting glowing ghostly footprints making their way across the floor. **BELOW:** Carrying on a long-standing tradition, Imagineer Adam Hill works on a scale model of the new Endless Staircase scene.

THE ENDLESS HALLWAY

"Every room has wall-to-wall creeps and hot and cold running chills. . . ."

ARRIVING ON THE "SECOND FLOOR," the Doom Buggies rotate slightly to point guests down what appears to be an endless hallway. Halfway down this corridor to infinity, a candelabra floats gracefully in midair, its three flickering candles lighting the way for one of the Mansion's 999 residents. A large armchair and a suit of armor stand near the Doom Buggy's path, both keeping their eyes on their houseguests. Is this haunted suit of armor actually moving, or is it your imagination?

THE CANDELABRA ACTUALLY "FLOATS" a short distance down the hallway, within a creation of forced perspective, one of the oldest tricks in the Imagineering book. A few feet behind the candelabra stands a full-length mirror, which creates the illusion of an endless corridor. The back of the candelabra is painted black to help minimize its reflection in the mirror. In addition to the scene's low lighting level, guests' view of the reflection and the other effects is further obscured by a thin black scrim that stretches across the hallway a few feet in front of the candelabra, which also contributes to the corridor's misty quality.

If you look closely, you will also be able to make out a face in the decorative pattern on the chair. Eagle-eyed guests are able to spot many such eyes and faces throughout the Mansion, most notably in the nearby Corridor of Doors. This was part of the Imagineers' effort to make guests feel as though they are constantly being watched, as well as create the sense that the house is alive.

ABOVE: The Endless Hallway at Walt Disney World. **BELOW LEFT:** The "face" in the chair is clearly visible in this design drawing. **BELOW RIGHT:** A scale model of the Endless Hallway, complete with flickering light fixtures and candelabra.

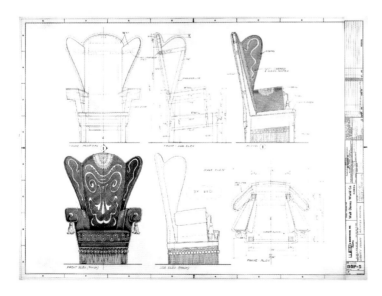

 THE BRIDE'S
WELCOME AND THE
ENDLESS HALLWAY

Shortly after leaving the Load Area at Phantom Manor, guests encounter the Bride for the first time. She bows gracefully as the Doom Buggies glide past her into the gloom. Seconds later, the Doom Buggies turn a bend to reveal the Endless Hallway, but with a new twist. The Bride stands midway down the corridor, then quickly disappears, leaving the candelabra she had been holding floating in midair—just as it does in the other Haunted Mansions. In terms of the story, it looks as though she is trying to warn guests away from proceeding down the Endless Hallway and supports the notion of an ongoing conflict between the Bride and the Phantom.

LEFT AND BELOW: Concept renderings for Phantom Manor indicate where guests first encounter the spectral ghost of Melanie Ravenswood. Imagineers felt it would contribute more to the Phantom Manor story line if the bride was momentarily visible, holding the floating candelabra in the Endless Hallway.

THE CONSERVATORY

"All our ghosts have been dying to meet you. This one can hardly contain himself."

THE DOOM BUGGIES GLIDE into the Conservatory, where a somewhat premature funeral is taking place. A large coffin sits at the side, surrounded by decaying floral arrangements. Two gnarled hands protrude from within the coffin, desperately trying to push the lid off and allow the undead (or is he?) occupant to escape. A cawing raven makes its perch near the coffin, seemingly warning guests not to disturb the corpse. The conservatory's expansive windows overlook a moonlit, fog-enshrouded landscape, providing an appropriately sinister backdrop for the scene.

SHOW WRITER X. ATENCIO himself supplied the voices for the corpse trapped in the coffin (as well as the attraction's emergency "Please Remain Seated" spiel).

The scene also marks the first appearance of the Raven—X.'s first choice for the Ghost Host—who would go on to become the attraction's unofficial spokesbird.

💀 THE MUSIC ROOM

Phantom Manor combines the Music Room and Conservatory from Walt Disney World scenes to create a new Music Room. This time it is a piano, not a coffin, that occupies the old conservatory, and a ghostly pianist plays a funereal version of "Grim Grinning Ghosts." The silhouette spilling across the floor is actually the Phantom. The Music Room opens onto the cacophonous Corridor of Doors.

OPPOSITE BOTTOM: Show Writer X. Atencio provided the plaintive wailing of a corpse trying to escape its coffin. OPPOSITE TOP: For Phantom Manor, the "premature funeral" was moved to the Underworld and the Conservatory was replaced by a proper Victorian Music Room.

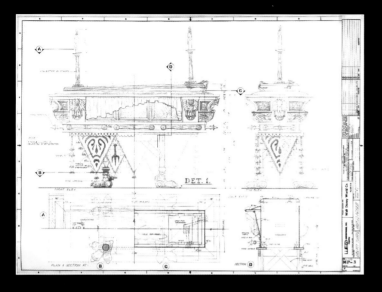

CLOCKWISE FROM TOP LEFT: Imagineers cover all the angles in this technical drawing of the coffin; The Raven was a featured performer from the very beginning, as seen in this early Ken Anderson concept rendering; The Conservatory's origins are evident in this X. Atencio concept rendering; The Music Room at Phantom Manor; The infamous Raven makes its first appearance perched to the left of the coffin in the Conservatory.

THE CORRIDOR OF DOORS

" ... they all seem to have trouble getting through. ... "

THE SPIRITS BEGIN TO GROW more restless and make their presence known as the Doom Buggies glide down the long Corridor of Doors. Doorknobs and handles twist and turn every which way, and knockers in the shape of spiked maces bang against their doors—by themselves. Unseen presences pound unmercifully on doors from the other side. Otherworldly creatures snarl, growl, howl, moan, and groan, dying to get out into the hallway. A pair of monstrous hands grips one door in a relentless attempt to break it open. Another door even appears to breathe, bulging out as a powerful force acts upon it from within the room. Some of the entities are not confined to their rooms: countless bestial eyes glare at guests from the corridor's sinister wallpaper.

THE CORRIDOR OF DOORS IS ONE of the darker and scarier regions of The Haunted Mansion, and clearly shows the influence of Claude Coats. His design of the corridor and many of its effects, the "breathing" door in particular, were heavily influenced by a film that came out during the attraction's long development, Robert Wise's 1963 classic thriller *The Haunting,* based on *The Haunting of Hill House* by Shirley Jackson.

The eyes and faces in the wallpaper also reflect *The Haunting's* influence, reinforcing the sense that the mansion itself is watching the guests. Although the signature purple-and-black pattern is often incorrectly credited to Marc Davis, it is actually Rolly Crump, with the guiding hand of Claude Coats, Rolly says, who created the eerie decoration; the wallpaper's look is typical of the designs he developed for his "Museum of the Weird."

TOP: In this view of the wall in the Corridor of Doors, the eerie Rolly Crump wallpaper further contributes to the sense that the house is "watching" its guests, even more so in the Walt Disney World version of the attraction following the 2007 enhancement **(BOTTOM). CENTER:** A formal portrait of still another one of Marc Davis's creepy creations hangs on the wall in Disneyland and now Walt Disney World. Many of the other pictures on the Corridor walls are actually framed images of the Hatbox Ghost, the skeletal Hitchhiker and the "pop-up" ghosts that appear in the Graveyard.

The Grandfather Clock

As the Doom Buggies leave the Corridor of Doors they pass by an ornate grandfather clock that is perpetually striking thirteen. The hour and minute hands spin madly around the face as the shadow of a claw passes over the clock. The moving shadow is one of the simplest effects in The Haunted Mansion: a silhouette of a claw rotating in front of a lighting fixture.

LEFT AND INSET: The devil is in the details. If you peer closely into the gloomy darkness, you can see that the top half of the cabinet is actually the head of a demon, the clock's face sitting inside its gaping maw, and the swinging pendulum is the demon's forked tongue.

ENHANCEMENTS
Knight of the Living Dead

In the mid-1980s, Imagineers grew concerned that Disneyland was becoming predictable and began looking for ways to add a few surprises to the park's signature attractions, including The Haunted Mansion. They teamed up with Entertainment to populate the Mansion with live performers for the first time, including a Phantom of the Opera–like character that would roam the queue and greet guests at the front door, and a "living" suit of armor in the Corridor of Doors. The idea was for these characters to pop up in different places at different times, adding a decidedly unpredictable element to the attraction.

This grand experiment proved to be a little too scary for guests . . . and a little too dangerous for Cast Members. Some guests were so surprised by the knight's sudden appearance that they unwittingly struck back at him. Unfortunately, the knight's armor wasn't quite as protective as that of his medieval predecessors, and his appearances met an untimely end.

SÉANCE CIRCLE

"Perhaps Madame Leota can establish contact. She has a remarkable head for materializing the disembodied."

WITH THE THIRTEEN CHIMES of the grandfather clock still ringing in the air, the Doom Buggies glide into Séance Circle, a dark sanctum in which an age-old ritual is taking place. A mist-filled crystal ball floats high above a table littered with tarot cards. The infamous Raven sits perched atop a chair directly behind the table. A large, ancient tome, *Necronomicon: Book of the Dead*, rests on a nearby bookstand, opened to pages 1312 and 1313 and a spell that summons spirits back from limbo.

As the Doom Buggies slowly circle the table, guests come face to face with their medium, a disembodied spirit —Madame Leota—glowing within the crystal ball. She summons the Mansion's restless spirits and encourages them to appear by reciting plaintive incantations: "Serpents and spiders, tail of a rat. Call in the spirits, wherever they're at." Musical instruments and other objects spin lazily through the air, as a wispy spirit begins to materialize in a far corner of the room.

MADAME LEOTA IS ONE OF THE MOST effective and convincing illusions in The Haunted Mansion, and yet is as simple as it is ingenious. This unique illusion dates back to early experiments Rolly Crump and Yale Gracey did in 1959. They took footage of character actor Hans Conried as the face in the Magic Mirror that had been shot for a Disney TV show and projected it onto a bust of Beethoven just to see what would happen. As Rolly recalls, "It wasn't really synced up right, but it did look like Beethoven was talking to you. We brought Walt down and showed it to him and he loved it."

The voice of Madame Leota was provided by another Disney veteran, Eleanor Audley, also heard as Cinderella's wicked stepmother and the evil Maleficent in *Sleeping Beauty*.

Madame Leota's face is actually that of WED model builder Leota Toombs. Imagineers shot footage of Leota performing to the audio tracks. Leota's face and Eleanor's voice were then combined, magically conjuring up the mysterious medium in all her ghostly glory. To this day, Imagineers commonly refer to the illusion as the "Leota Effect," a tribute to the immortal Ms. Toombs and the disembodied spirit she helped bring to afterlife.

TOP: To create the immortal character of Madame Leota, Imagineers combined the face of fellow employee Leota Toombs (**ABOVE**), seen here working on a model for Country Bear Jamboree, with the distinctive voice of Eleanor Audley (**LEFT**).

ENHANCEMENTS
Floating Leota

The "floating Leota" effect made its debut in 2005 in Disneyland—initially conceived as one of the ways to "refresh the classics" for the Park's golden anniversary—and two years later in Walt Disney World. The gag is truly the twenty-first-century equivalent of the original Leota effect, made even more magical by its seemingly impossible flight through the darkness of Séance Circle.

The open spell book contains a couple of hidden details for eagle-eyed fans. The scythe-wielding Death figure is actually a cloaked version of the skeletal Hitchhiking Ghost (or the Hatbox Ghost, who shares the same look); the spell itself is the same one actor Dean Jones recites when he inadvertently calls forth Peter Ustinov as the titular Blackbeard's Ghost in the 1967 Walt Disney film. That bit of black magic is followed by Madame Leota's incantations in their entirety.

TOP LEFT: Chris Turner rendering of the Floating Leota show enhancement. **TOP:** This scale model illustrates how the Doom Buggies move through the original Séance scene along a circular length of track. **ABOVE:** Another early concept rendering shows a more skeletal medium for the séance scene. **BELOW:** In this storyboard of Phantom Manor's Séance Circle, the conjured spirits themselves are visible through a series of archways.

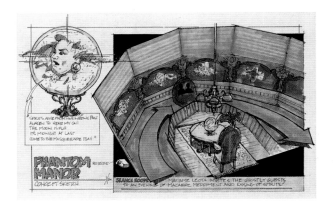

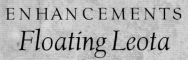

 In Phantom Manor, Séance Circle looks more like a formal Victorian sitting room than a dark realm of shadows, complete with a number of curtained archways through which guests can see spirits "materialize" and glide through the darkness. The scene lacks the floating musical instruments of its predecessors, and Madame Leota's incantations (delivered alternatively in both French and English) reference the Bride and foreshadow a wedding party.

THE GRAND HALL

"The happy haunts have received your sympathetic vibrations and are beginning to materialize...."

T HE DOOM BUGGIES LEAVE Séance Circle and travel onto a balcony overlooking the aptly named Grand Hall. A group of otherworldly revelers have gathered at a long banquet table to celebrate a swinging wake. The guests slowly fade in and out of sight, seemingly in time with the hostess's repeated attempts to extinguish the candles on a "death-day" cake. Other swinging specters enjoy spirits of a different kind while sitting atop an ornate chandelier high above the table. Wispy wraiths fly in and out of the room through the upper windows as lightning flashes behind them. And a steady stream of ghostly guests pours in from a hearse parked just outside the hall, eager to join the fun.

At the opposite end of the hall, couples dance the night away as an organist plays "Grim Grinning Ghosts," this time arranged as a waltz, on an enormous pipe organ. Screaming skulls, not musical notes, can be seen pouring from the pipes and vanishing into thin air. On a wall above the dance floor hang the portraits of two pistol-wielding duelists. Their spirits emerge from the portraits in an eternal attempt to settle their score long after their deaths. It is truly a party to die for.

THE SCENE IS A DIRECT DESCENDANT of the ghostly wedding reception seen in an early piece of Claude Coats's concept art. The "Great Caesar's Ghost" character called for in one of Ken Anderson's early treatments even puts in an appearance, seated at one end of the banquet table. Look closely underneath the table for another partygoer who is resting in peace. And if you check out the mantel above the fireplace, you'll see a ghost seated next to a marble bust of the very same stern-looking schoolmarm that appears in the Portrait Corridor.

Contrary to popular belief and urban legend, it is not holograms, sophisticated laser effects, or even real ghosts that populate the Grand Hall. The scene is a true showcase for the art of Audio-Animatronics and illusions that Rolly and Yale had been experimenting with since 1959. In fact, the Grand Hall scene is the world's largest working application of the Pepper's Ghost effect, named after its inventor, John Henry Pepper, a professor of chemistry at the London Polytechnic Institute, who developed the illusion in 1862 for use in the theater. It works based on the fact that viewers can see objects *through* glass and objects reflected *off* glass at the exact same time.

"We actually had professional magicians come out, and we did the Pepper's Ghost for them," Rolly recalls. "We fooled them, too, because they had never seen a piece of glass that big before."

The biggest challenge for the Imagineers was to position the Audio-Animatronics figures so they would line up accurately with the props on the set. "There's one technical boo-boo in it," X. Atencio told *Storyboard* magazine. "The dancers are dancing backward. The gal is leading the guy. It's animated the right way, but with the mirror image it becomes backward."

OPPOSITE BOTTOM: The Grand Hall, in which, according to the Ghost Host, the happy haunts are "assembling for a swinging wake." **OPPOSITE INSET:** The ghosts in the Grand Hall are an illusion created using the "Pepper's Ghost" effect, an effect popular in turn-of-the-century theatrical presentations.

ABOVE: A three-dimensional version of a Portrait Corridor bust makes an appearance in the Grand Hall, as seen in this Marc Davis concept. **BELOW:** An "alternate angle" by Marc Davis, in which ghostly guests can be seen emerging from a hearse and entering the Grand Hall.

ABOVE, LEFT TO RIGHT: Marc Davis's original concept drawings of the duelists were adapted into full-size oil paintings located in the Grand Hall. LEFT: The "grandmother" in the rocking chair made her first appearance (in her "mortal state") in Walt Disney's Carousel of Progress. BELOW: Audio-Animatronics partygoers include Great Caesar's Ghost.

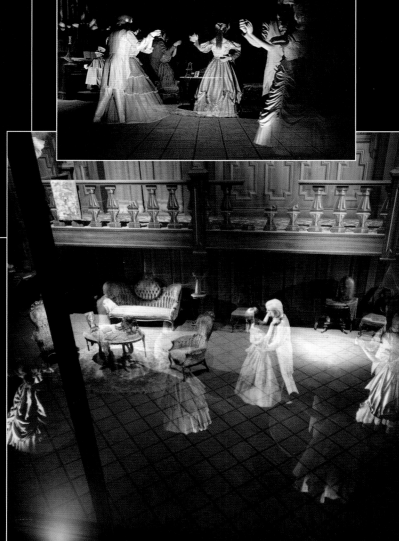

TOP RIGHT: High spirits. **CENTER AND RIGHT:** A series of rare views of the Grand Hall and its otherworldly occupants. **ABOVE:** The organist strikes a pose that does not actually appear in the attraction.

ABOVE: Concept art of the Grand Hall duelists. **RIGHT AND FAR RIGHT:** The Audio-Animatronic figures from Pirates of the Caribbean, and their designer, Blaine Gibson. **BELOW:** Concept art of the ghost "Pickwick" and friends on the Grand Hall chandelier.

A CLOSER LOOK at the pistol-wielding duelists emerging from their portraits reveals them to be Audio-Animatronics refugees from Pirates of the Caribbean, including the infamous Auctioneer himself.

THE GHOST SWINGING from the top of the chandelier is the only character other than Madame Leota referred to by a specific name—Pickwick—in Walt Disney Imagineering show documentation. The moniker can likely be attributed to the character's decidedly Dickensian appearance. But could it also have something to do with the fact that many of the in-joke–loving Imagineers drove past a banquet hall called the Pickwick Center every day on their way to the WED campus in Glendale? The world may never know for sure.

THE ORGAN IN THE GRAND HALL scene at
Disneyland is actually Captain Nemo's pipe organ
(minus the pipes) from 20,000 *Leagues Under the Sea*.
The instrument was repainted and refitted with a
bat-shaped music stand and other ghostly details.
The organs in the subsequent Haunted Mansions
are exact reproductions of the Disneyland original.

TOP LEFT: Marc Davis rendering of the organist. **ABOVE:** Captain Nemo's organ in its new home. **LEFT:** Ken Anderson's wedding party finally welcomes guests in Phantom Manor's version of the Grand Hall scene.

 Phantom Manor's Grand Hall depicts a
formal wedding party celebrating the
Bride's imminent nuptials, just as the
scene was originally intended for The
Haunted Mansion in an early Claude Coats rendering. Although most of the scene is staged in exactly
the same way as its American and Japanese counterparts, here the Bride stands halfway up the staircase,
greeting guests disembarking from a hearse parked
outside. Brilliant lightning flashes reveal the
silhouette of the Phantom in the window above the
staircase, his evil laughter ringing out over the
revelry. As the scene continues, everyone slowly
disappears except for the Bride, a melancholy
reminder that her wedding never took place . . .
and a chilling premonition of things to come.

THE ATTIC

"Till death . . . do us part."

LEAVING THE GRAND HALL, the Doom Buggies carry guests into the Mansion's dusty attic, which is filled with bric-a-brac, lamps, and long-stored gifts and mementos from weddings that took place more than a century ago. Cool blue light and the sound of a beating heart permeate the space, and the ominous atmosphere is underscored by the sounds of a piano that plays a rather dismal version of Richard Wagner's "Bridal Chorus."

The wedding gifts include crystal, china, candelabra, music boxes, household goods, some men's clothing, wedding albums, and guest books. The gifts become grander with each successive marriage Prominently displayed among all the curios and keepsakes are several formal wedding portraits of a presumably happy bride and groom. Guests immediately notice that the same beautiful young woman appears in all the portraits—but with a different groom in each one; the bride clearly gains in wealth and social stature with each wedding. She wears the same wedding dress in each portrait, but adds a strand of pearls for each subsequent marriage. Even more disquieting, each husband's head disappears temporarily from his body, only to reappear seconds later.

Then guests encounter a luminous, floating apparition of the bride, Constance, who has manifested herself in the attic. She glows in the light as her bridal gown and veil flutter in a ghostly breeze. As she repeats her

vows ("In sickness . . . and in wealth!"), a razor-sharp ax materializes in her hands, glinting in the moonlight. The "Black Widow Bride" offers a sinister smile, the ax disappears, and she recites another of her favorite vows in a haunting voice: "Till Death Do Us Part. . . ."

The Doom Buggies exit through the attic window.

CONSTANCE, THE "BLACK WIDOW BRIDE" as she came to be known at Imagineering, first materialized in May 2006 in Disneyland and September 2007 in Walt Disney World. The bride's sinister story was penned by show writer Chris Goosman, who deepened the veteran Mansion character by turning her into a gold digging seductress with a taste for the finer things. The portraits and wedding gifts tell the story of the way Constance improved her station through each of her five marriages, culminating in her wedding to one of the mansion's many owners. Chris deliberately named the fifth and final groom George, and the Imagineer playing him (all of the ill-fated grooms were Imagineers) was made up to resemble George Patecleaver, the "axed"

LEFT: The first portrait shows young Constance towering over her groom, Ambrose, the naïve but good-intentioned son of successful farmers. The decidedly innocent-looking Ambrose is pictured wearing an unfashionable bowler hat and a "sensible" but ill-fitting woolen suit. The cover of their wedding book heralds:

OUR WEDDING DAY

Ambrose and Constance

1869

RIGHT: Constance's second marriage was to Frank, an eastern banker and a pillar of his community. Sharp-eyed guests will note that all of the wedding-gifts tableaux depict a bride and headless groom in some form or fashion. Among the wedding gifts on display in this vignette is a porcelain figure of an elegant eighteenth-century Frenchwoman, who stands over the toppled figure of a French man, whose head apparently snapped off in the fall. A Victorian-style banner adorned with cupids, hearts, and flowers prematurely announces:

Constance and Frank

TRUE LOVE FOREVER

LEFT: Moving ever onward and upward, the Black Widow Bride's third husband was a foreign diplomat known as the Marquis. He was photographed in full military dress uniform with a ribbon draped from shoulder to waist and a jacket sporting a number of medals, a testament to his rarified station in life, topped off by a formal hat complete with regal plume. Near the portrait stands a hat rack, upon which hangs a hat from each of Constance's five husbands.

The Marquis and Constance

1874

RIGHT: Constance's penultimate husband, as she continued her ascent of the social ladder, was Reginald, a celebrated railroad baron, gambler, and world-renown gourmand. In a manner befitting his lofty position in life, Reginald sports the brocade vest, lacy shirt, formal jacket, and classic top hat of a distinguished gentleman. An enormous ring conspicuously adorns his little finger. The Black Widow Bride's diabolical plot is unfolding exactly as planned.

Reginald and Constance

1875

LEFT: Constance's fifth and final marriage was to George, one of the owners of the manor house that would later come to be known as The Haunted Mansion. With his bushy mustache and deep-set eyes, he is unmistakable as the man who, in later years, would be depicted in one of the stretching portraits, his grim visage etched upon a tombstone. The wedding gifts on display are the most ornate of all, including crystal bowls, vases, and imported china. A number of souvenirs from some of George's exotic foreign trips can also be seen in this vignette. The wedding portrait appears in a large, decorative frame and includes the inscription:

George and Constance

husband depicted on a tombstone in the Stretch Room portrait, as named in a 1968 X. Atencio show script. That said, in the earlier script it is "Widow Abigale Patecleaver, who was preceded by her husband," and not Constance – who clearly died young – depicted in that same elongated portrait.

Imagineers used a higher-tech version of the classic Leota effect to create Constance. They even continued the tradition of having two different performers play one character: actress Julia Lee physically portrayed the Bride, while veteran voice-over artist Kat Cressida supplied her voice.

TOP: This vignette depicts Constance's ill-fated second marriage to Frank, whose grim fate is preserved forever in an eerie, transforming portrait. **ABOVE:** Chris Runco's concept sketch of the same scene illustrates how each prop and piece of set dressing helps tell the story of Constance, the Black Widow Bride.

THE BRIDE'S BOUDOIR

A trip through the Bride's Boudoir replaces the Attic as the final scene inside Phantom Manor. The Phantom watches over the Bride as she sits at her makeup table, eternally preparing for a wedding that will never take place. The image in the looking glass is not her own but that of a misty skull, as though the mirror is offering the Bride a glimpse of her fate.

LEFT: The Bride's Boudoir at Phantom Manor. **INSET:** Concept art of the Bride in her boudoir at Phantom Manor.

TOP: A Marc Davis concept rendering of the Hatbox Ghost, with and without cloak. CENTER: A scale model showing the Hatbox Ghost occupying the space where his Bride now stands. ABOVE: The Hatbox Ghost figure as it was originally installed. RIGHT: Yale Gracey making adjustments to what is likely a prototype Hatbox Ghost.

The Hatbox Ghost

In a departure from some of Ken Anderson's early stories, Imagineers did not originally plan to leave the bride stranded at the altar. For a short period of time she did have a groom—the infamous Hatbox Ghost, whose very existence fans have theorized and argued about for years. This sinister groom character did, indeed, exist, but unfortunately for the bride, the honeymoon was over before it could even begin.

"He was originally going to be where the bride is now," Imagineer Tony Baxter explains. "The bride was going to be in the exact opposite corner. In fact, for years, the Doom Buggy turned you directly that way so you could see her, but there was nothing to see because we had moved her to the other end of the attic. Now, that spot is occupied by the playing harpsichord. The Hatbox Ghost just disappeared—the molds, the figure itself, everything, so all we have are photos and renderings."

But why? Was he just too frightening? Was it his chilling visage that caused a reporter to have a heart attack, to tie him into another unfounded urban legend? The true story isn't nearly as ghoulish. The Hatbox Ghost effect simply didn't work.

As originally planned, the Hatbox Ghost stood near the Attic's exit, leaning on a cane in his right hand and holding a hatbox aloft in the left. "With every beat of his bride's heart, his head disappeared from his body . . . and reappeared in the hatbox," as it was described

in *The Story and Song from The Haunted Mansion.* The illusion was created by a carefully timed lighting effect. The standing ghost's head was illuminated by black light, and the head in the hatbox was lit with a small, pin spotlight. When the black light faded down and the pin spot came up, it did, indeed, look as though his head had vanished and reappeared inside the hatbox. The effect was then reversed on the next beat of the bride's heart.

Due to the guests' proximity to the figure and the Attic's ambient light, it could never be dark enough for the effect to be truly convincing. The speed at which the Doom Buggies moved by the figure also ensured that there could never be enough time to run the entire gag. Although the Hatbox Ghost appeared during Cast Member previews and possibly even a soft opening to the general public, the figure was removed before the attraction's official debut, never to be seen again.

THE GRAVEYARD

"When the crypt doors creak and the tombstones quake,
Spooks come out for a swinging wake."

A FTER PASSING THE LOVELORN BRIDE, the Doom Buggies "fall" out an attic window (though guests are still safely inside the show building), all under the watchful, glowing red eyes of the Raven perched in a nearby tree.

"Grim Grinning Ghosts," this time arranged as a jazzy jamboree, fills the air once again as the Doom Buggies pass a terrified caretaker and his hound dog and drift into a graveyard at the side of the Mansion. Guests encounter what appear to be hundreds of ghosts rising from their graves in a tour de force of Marc Davis character designs and sight gags. The spirits cross all boundaries of space and time, from a band of medieval minstrels and a Victorian-era king and queen balancing on a teeter-totter to a properly paranormal English tea party and an Egyptian mummy sitting in an open sarcophagus. All are singing and playing along with their hosts for the evening's festivities, a group of warbling marble busts. Madame Leota's incantations have worked like a charm, and all of the Mansion's 999 happy haunts have "come out to socialize" at last.

TOP RIGHT: The Caretaker's expression gives guests an idea of what lies ahead in the Graveyard. **RIGHT AND BELOW:** Marc Davis's light touch is evident in these concept renderings of characters and gags for The Haunted Mansion's grand finale.

There are more Audio-Animatronics figures in the Graveyard than any other scene in the attraction. Many were built without the layer of "skin" common to Disney's mortal characters, and wear costumes made of a semitransparent, raincoatlike material, giving them an appropriately translucent, skeletal appearance. Other figures are accented by fluorescent-colored paint, props, and clothing, all of which glow brightly under the scene's black light. In addition to these Audio-Animatronics apparitions, a number of Rolly and Yale's "pop-up ghosts" are strategically placed throughout the Graveyard.

The Imagineers once again used forced perspective to make the Graveyard appear to be much larger than it actually is. Props and set pieces get smaller the farther away they are. Separate pieces of thin theatrical scrim hang between the Omnimover track and the set's rear walls, which provide an even greater sense of depth and help create an eerie, foglike atmosphere.

TOP: One of the graveyard's ubiquitous "pop-up" ghosts, with Marc Davis's headless knight and opera singers visible in the background. **ABOVE:** The merry minstrels as they appear in the finished attraction. **ABOVE RIGHT:** A knight and his executioner show there are no hard feelings as they sing "Grim Grinning Ghosts" together. A bearded convict, who will soon attempt to hitch a ride with guests, stands nearby. **RIGHT:** These close-ups illustrate the translucent costumes, fluorescent colors, and black lighting that give the graveyard ghosts their distinctive look.

MANY GUESTS HAVE WONDERED how Imagineers created the "Night on Bald Mountain"–style illusion of myriad ghosts rising from their graves upon entering the Graveyard. While it may not be surprising to learn that it is a projection effect onto a scrim, the story behind it may prove to be a bit of a shock.

When Yale Gracey and Rolly Crump were experimenting with the projection of Hans Conried as the Magic Mirror, they inadvertently beamed his face onto a party hall standard—a rotating mirror ball. To their amazement, thousands of images of Conried's face were sent swirling around the room. Yale and Rolly knew immediately that they could adapt this amazing effect to create some of their 999 happy haunts and they did—as the rising spirits in the Graveyard.

ABOVE: Wispy spirits can be seen rising from their graves in this Collin Campbell concept drawing. **RIGHT:** "Now You Sea Him": At Walt Disney World, the infamous Sea Captain sits on a tombstone drinking tea to the right of the hearse.

The Singing Busts

The Singing Busts in the Graveyard scene are dubbed "The Phantom Five" and led by the character of "Uncle Theodore," played by Thurl Ravenscroft, also known as the original voice of Tony the Tiger and the baritone who sung "You're a Mean One, Mr. Grinch" in *How the Grinch Stole Christmas!* Contrary to another inexplicably popular urban legend, none of the faces belongs to Walt Disney. The rest of the Phantom Five is composed of (left to right) Rollo Rumkin (Verne Rowe), Uncle Theodore, Cousin Algernon (Chuck Schroeder), Ned Nub (Jay Meyer), and Phineas P. Pock (Bob Ebright).

The illusion of the Singing Busts is created through the same effect used in the séance scene. Singing along to a playback of "Grim Grinning Ghosts," the performers could use only their eyes and mouths to "sell" the song, which explains their exaggerated, almost cartoon-like facial expressions.

ABOVE: Jay Meyer provided the face for Ned Nub, one of the singing busts that appear in the Graveyard scene. **RIGHT:** A Marc Davis concept rendering. **BELOW:** A scale model.

INTO THE UNDERWORLD

In one of Phantom Manor's most drastic departures from the original Haunted Mansion, the Gothic cemetery finale is traded for a more exotic "descent into the Underworld," a journey that culminates in the dusty streets of a literal ghost town. Gliding out of the Bride's Boudoir and onto the Manor's garden terrace, the Phantom himself invites guests to join him on the other side. As if on cue, the Doom Buggies fall backward into an open grave that the Phantom has freshly dug just for the occasion. Guests descend beneath Boot Hill cemetery, where all sorts of ghosts, ghouls, and goblins rise from their graves. Decaying corpses begin to reanimate and a troupe of skeletons dances along to "Grim Grinning Ghosts," which is performed by a quartet of crumbling marble busts. The dancing skeletons were inspired by Walt Disney's 1929 Silly Symphony, *The Skeleton Dance*.

Phantom Canyon

The Phantom's hideous laughter fills the air as the Doom Buggies emerge from the catacombs into a ghostly version of Thunder Mesa, here known as Phantom Canyon. Guests pass the train station, complete with passing ghost train, and head into town. The rickety wooden walls of the town begin to shake, rattle, and roll as guests relive that fateful earthquake of 1860. The ride rolls right down the ghost town's main drag, where the mayor is tipping his hat—and his head—to welcome guests. This is the only time The Haunted Mansion's original narration and the voice of Paul Frees can be heard in Phantom Manor. Guests are treated to supernatural versions of Western-movie staples, including a ghostly poker game, an old-fashioned shoot-out, and even a bank robbery in progress.

ABOVE: The Phantom is on hand to welcome guests as they leave Ravenswood Manor and begin their descent into the Underworld in this concept design by Fernando Tenedora.

TOP, LEFT AND RIGHT: The crowd-pleasing singing busts, reduced to a quartet, make the move underground as illustrated in the concept rendering. **ABOVE AND LEFT:** Decaying corpses reanimate and rise from their graves as Doom Buggies carry guests ever deeper into the catacombs beneath Phantom Manor.

The Underworld gives way to Phantom Canyon, a night-marish image of Thunder Mesa populated by all manner of decaying corpses as seen in these concept renderings and photographs.

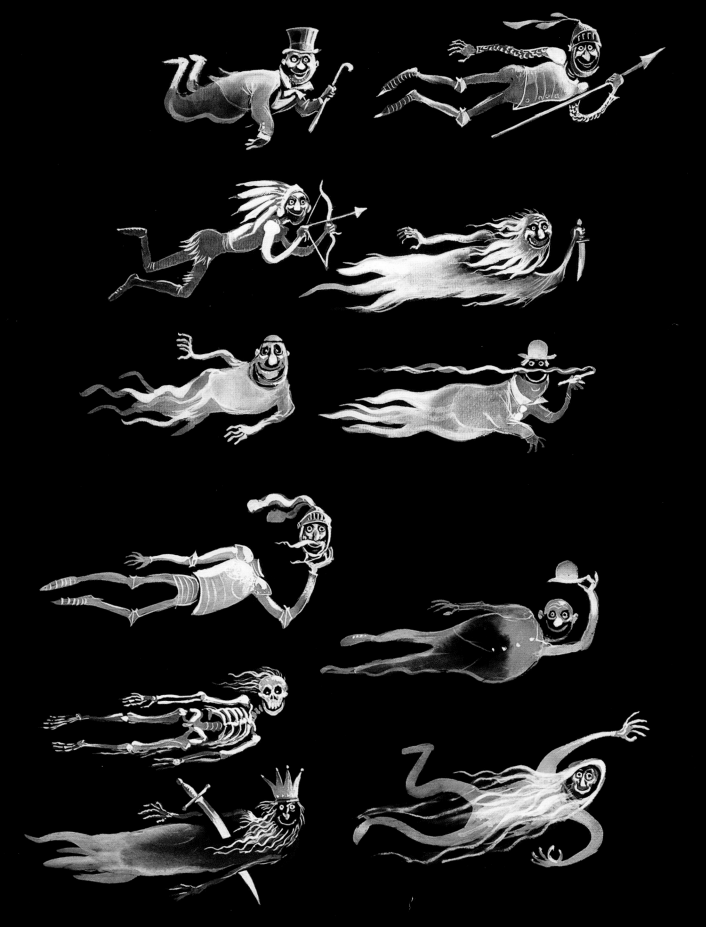

THE CRYPT

HE RAVEN PUTS IN ONE LAST appearance, glaring at guests with its glowing red eyes as they enter a giant stone crypt. "There's a little matter I forgot to mention," the Ghost Host adds as guests come face-to-face with the Mansion's most popular characters. "Beware of hitchhiking ghosts!"

ALTHOUGH THE HITCHHIKING GHOSTS do not have official names, fans and Cast Members alike have come to know them by unofficial monikers that are now so widely accepted they were used in early drafts of *The Haunted Mansion* movie script. From left to right, Phineas is the large ghost in a top hat carrying a carpetbag; Ezra is the tall, bony ghost tipping his hat; and Gus is the short convict with a bushy beard and the ball and chain.

As popular as they turned out to be, surprisingly, the Hitchhiking Ghosts only *just* made it into the attraction's final design. As X. Atencio told *Storyboard* magazine, "It was kind of an afterthought, though. It didn't come until the ride was practically put in there." The appearance of the hitchhikers changed dramatically throughout the design process. Cartoonlike in Marc Davis's earliest sketches, they took on a much more realistic appearance as they made their way from page to stage.

"...And a Ghost Will Follow You Home...."

The Doom Buggies continue deeper into the Crypt, where they pass in front of a series of large mirrors. Guests quickly discover that one of the three ghosts has hitched a ride and is seated next to them.

There is no Hitchhiking Ghost in the mirror, of course, but that is simply because guests are not looking into a mirror. The ghost in the Doom Buggy is another Pepper's Ghost illusion, but, unlike the Grand Hall scene, this time the ghosts are real and the guests are the reflection.

Rolly Crump's influence can be seen one more time in the form of flickering torches held by faux human hands, which are attached to the stone wall next to the mirrors. "I was influenced by some avant-garde French films, like Cocteau's *Beauty and the Beast*," Rolly recalls. "There were all these human body parts that were part of the architecture and came to life. I thought, Hey, that's neat! So I started doing human body parts as part of the architecture."

OPPOSITE: Marc Davis concept renderings of a variety of Hitchhiking Ghosts, some of which were adapted into characters for other show scenes. **ABOVE:** Going our way? **BELOW:** Rolly Crump's Cocteau-inspired design lends a helping hand.

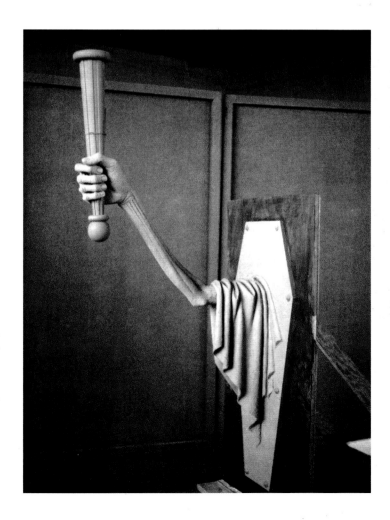

 As the Doom Buggies head out of town, the Phantom and the Bride both make one last play for their guests' souls. The cackling Phantom gestures to an open coffin, inviting guests to make Phantom Canyon their permanent home. But the Bride, now a leering skeleton in a tattered wedding dress, comes to their rescue once again, appearing within a swirling vortex of color and light to point the way to safety.

Proceeding back into the Manor, guests note a series of ornate mirrors hanging upon the wall. This time, instead of a Hitchhiking Ghost materializing beside guests, the Phantom himself is seen creeping over the top of the vehicle in one last attempt to keep them in the Manor forever. The creative team felt this approach was more effective than the original—after all, you can look inside your Doom Buggy at The Haunted Mansions and see that there is no Hitchhiking Ghost next to you. But you *can't* see the top of the vehicle at Phantom Manor to confirm whether or not the Phantom is there. Effective—and creepy.

ABOVE: Guests get into the act as they become an integral part of the Pepper's Ghost illusion in one of The Haunted Mansion's most convincing and beloved gags. **BELOW:** The Phantom's last stand is visible in this concept rendering of the Disneyland Paris version of the infamous mirror gag.

The many forms of the Hitchhiking Ghosts. BELOW: A Marc Davis concept rendering. CENTER: A scale model. BOTTOM: Finished Audio-Animatronics figures under show conditions.

TOP: A Blaine Gibson clay sculpture (sans wardrobe). ABOVE LEFT: A close view of "Phineas" as he appears "through the looking glass." ABOVE RIGHT: Imagineers definitely know how to use their heads. "Ezra" makes a few additional "unbilled" appearances in The Haunted Mansion. His head—with its signature bulging eyes and wide, leering grin—is used in a number of the "pop-up" ghost gags throughout the attraction.

LITTLE LEOTA

"Hurry ba-ack . . . hurry ba-ack. Be sure to bring your death certificate if you decide to join us. Make final arrangements now. We've been dying to have you."

ONE LAST SPIRIT BECKONS to guests as they ride a moving walkway out of the crypt. With this plaintive invitation still ringing in their ears, guests continue back to the relative safety of New Orleans Square.

THE TINY GHOST, STANDING ATOP the ledge of the crypt, holds a bouquet of flowers in her hand and stares wistfully into the distance. She is officially called the "Ghostess" (a combination of "ghost" and "hostess'), though most fans and Cast Members refer to her as "Little Leota," since she is portrayed by Leota Toombs of Madame Leota fame. This time, however, Ms. Toombs supplied both the character's face and her eerie voice, which have become a guest favorite over the years.

TOP: Guests encounter Little Leota after disembarking from their Doom Buggies, as seen in this scale model for the Disneyland attraction. **ABOVE:** The face *and* voice of Leota Toombs are immortalized in her role as "Little Leota." **LEFT:** A concept rendering of the Bride, who replaces Little Leota, and appears in the wine cellar of Phantom Manor.

THE MAUSOLEUM

Upon disembarking from their Doom Buggies at Florida and Tokyo, guests exit the Mansion through a Mausoleum as a faint, almost chantlike version of "Grim Grinning Ghosts" fills their ears. The epitaphs on the walls of the crypt are almost exclusively humorous, trading bad puns for references to Imagineers. There is even a reference to the oft-married fictional pirate, Bluebeard, another apparent tie-in to the early sea captain/bloodthirsty pirate story line. Guests emerge from the Mausoleum to find themselves back on the Mansion's grounds, a few short steps away from the entrance gate, safety—and a conveniently placed merchandise cart.

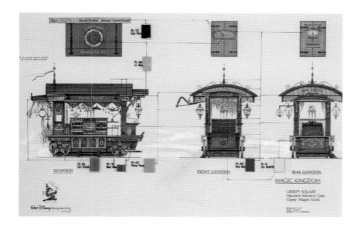

BOOT HILL

After stepping out from their Doom Buggies, Disneyland Paris guests emerge from the house to find themselves on Boot Hill, the Ravenswood family burial ground, which they discover was later opened up to all Thunder Mesa residents. Henry and Martha Ravenswood and members of their families are all buried here, along with members of some of Thunder Mesa's finest families. Guests also find that the Imagineers didn't stray too far from a cherished Disneyland tradition, and a quick look at the epitaphs proves that nobody in Thunder Mesa seemed to take death too seriously.

TOP: The Mausoleum as it appears at Walt Disney World and Tokyo Disneyland. **ABOVE LEFT:** A concept rendering of a Madame Leota–themed merchandise cart. **ABOVE RIGHT:** The final product as it appears outside The Haunted Mansion's gates at Walt Disney World. **LEFT:** "'Til death do us part?"–united forever in Phantom Manor's Boot Hill cemetery. **RIGHT:** Getting booted out of Phantom Manor.

Third Story
AT THE MOVIES

Introduction

MAYBE IT'S INEVITABLE that the world inside the front doors of The Haunted Mansion would eventually inspire an experience inside a movie theater. After all, the Mansion was designed by some of Hollywood's finest filmmakers, including Walt Disney himself. The combined stagecraft of these filmmakers made for one of the longest-running theatrical experiences anywhere. It's the best of cinema and animation and theater all rolled into one glorious piece of entertainment.

Before we started production on the film, we arranged with Disneyland to make an early morning trip to the Mansion before the park opened. It was about 7:00 A.M. when we walked through the deserted streets of New Orleans Square, a little afraid that by touring through the Mansion and seeing all the illusions close-up, it would forever spoil the experience for us. It had the opposite effect. Walking those hallowed haunted halls made us all appreciate the Mansion and its funny, twisted, masterful theatricality more than ever.

In a way, that early morning trip to Disneyland became a connection between two generations of filmmakers. It was a chance for artists, long separated by time or place, to have a reunion of the spirit. A chance for Ken Anderson to show his ideas to John Myhre. A chance for Marc Davis and Blaine Gibson to share their characters with Rick Baker. A chance for the great artists of the past to inspire us with their genius.

That visit was the beginning of hundreds of drawings, thousands of conversations, and endless, painstaking hours on a soundstage that would turn the legendary tales of the Mansion into a major motion picture. With the talents of an amazing cast and crew, and with visionary director Rob Minkoff as our host, The Haunted Mansion opens its doors once again to the magical, inexplicable, unbelievable world within.

DON HAHN
Producer, *The Haunted Mansion*

PRECEDING SPREAD: A preliminary and unfinished study of The Haunted Mansion as envisioned in its Southern bayou setting. **OPPOSITE:** Edward Gracey (Nathaniel Parker) carries his beloved Elizabeth (Marsha Thomason) out of a grand Mardi Gras ball during a crucial moment in *The Haunted Mansion*. **ABOVE:** Producer Don Hahn hitches a ride with some well-known friends.

The Haunted Mansion Goes Home

WALT DISNEY IMAGINEERING was born of the film industry. The first Imagineers were filmmakers handpicked by Walt Disney to translate stories from the two-dimensional world of the cinema into the three-dimensional world of the theme park, as well as create original concepts such as The Haunted Mansion. In this form, Walt could fully immerse his audience in sensory experiences rich with adventure, romance, comedy, and fear. Early in the twenty-first century, some of the original attraction concepts began a reverse journey to the cinematic world.

In early 2001, The Walt Disney Studios began recognizing the potential some of the theme park attractions had as film properties. Brigham Taylor, Vice President, Production, and in-house producer

Andrew Gunn looked for logical choices for big-screen treatments. During a visit they made together to Disneyland, Brigham suggested to Andrew, "You know, we should do a Haunted Mansion movie."

It was an inspired idea. The Haunted Mansion is a true legend among Disney fans around the world. The attraction's rich environments and memorable cast of characters made it a natural story for filmmakers—the original Imagineers—to tell. Brigham and Andrew brought the idea back to Nina Jacobson, President, Buena Vista Motion Pictures Group, who quickly agreed. "These attractions are deeply ingrained in our childhood memories," Nina affirms. "They also tell really wonderful stories." Jacobson's approval made it unanimous: The Haunted Mansion was going to the movies.

TOP, LEFT TO RIGHT: Haunted Mansion legends Marc Davis, Paul Frees, Blaine Gibson, and Thurl Ravenscroft were the inspiration for the film's Singing Busts, but only Frees and Ravenscroft would make the final cut. **LEFT:** Live actors are used to portray Audio-Animatronics figures, instead of the other way around, as seen in these images of the Grand Hall duelists and the Hitchhiking Ghosts.

"A DISQUIETING METAMORPHOSIS"

Brigham and Andrew knew from the beginning that they couldn't simply transcribe the attraction's script and film it. Much like adapting a novel, they had to treat the attraction as source material and figure out a way to make it work on film. "We looked at all the original story material at Walt Disney Imagineering," Andrew recalls. "The treatments, the artwork. We said, 'Let's use this and move on from here.'"

They turned to staff writer David Berenbaum to expand that original story material into a screenplay and he began to look for ways to work elements of the attraction in his script. "There were always ideas I knew would be in the movie, such as Madame Leota and the Hitchhiking Ghosts. And we always knew we wanted a family to spend a night in a haunted mansion," the writer recalls. "Once you put those flags in the ground, your story evolves from there. The fun part for me was taking the elements from the ride and making a solid narrative out of them, tipping our hat to the attraction but not being beholden to it.

"Leota was a main part of it," David continues. "I always thought she was a great character and a great way to give out portions of the mystery in a 'Disneyesque' way, in riddles and rhymes. The Hitchhiking Ghosts were prominent in early drafts, but were then trimmed back because it became too overwhelming to have three supporting characters chiming in all the time. There's a ballroom, the dancers from the eighteenth century, all the cemetery ghosts—you'll recognize everything from the attraction."

The writer spent several months working out the story, encountering several modifications along the way. The location shifted from upstate New York, the perfect setting for a Walt Disney World–style mansion, to the bayous of New Orleans, home of the original Disneyland attraction. Additionally, the main character evolved from an attorney handling the dispo-

ABOVE: Costume Designer Mona May's concept design for Nathaniel Parker as Edward Gracey. **BELOW:** Screenwriter David Berenbaum.

sition of an antebellum mansion into a workaholic real estate agent charged with trying to sell the old house.

Eventually, David rebuilt The Haunted Mansion from a seven-minute attraction into a feature film. As the story goes, Jim Evers, an ambitious real estate agent, seems to care more about making his next big deal than about his family: his wife and business partner, Sara, and their children, Megan and Michael. That all begins to change when Edward Gracey, the wealthy owner of an antebellum mansion on the edge of a remote bayou, requests Sara, and Sara alone, to come to his home and discuss handling its sale. Smelling the biggest deal of his career, Jim insists on tagging along, bringing their children with him. An unexpected thunderstorm strands the Evers family in the old mansion with the brooding Gracey, his mysterious butler, Ramsley, and a variety of unseen residents—according to Gracey's repeated claims that the house is haunted. Jim scoffs at Gracey's ghost stories, preferring to discuss razing the mansion and subdividing the land for condos. But not everything is as it seems, and the family slowly discovers that Sara may have an otherworldly connection to Edward Gracey and the mansion's dark past. When his wife and children mysteriously disappear, Jim, assisted by a certain disembodied spirit in a crystal ball, must

jim (o.s) "ovch! ovch!"

PAN

> SPLASH <

unlock the secrets of this haunted mansion and recognize just how important his family is in order to save them . . . and himself.

That central story line served as a foundation for the additional drafts of the script Berenbaum would write over the next two years. Subplots and entire scenes would come and go, but the basic premise remained very much the same throughout the screenplay's development. Much like the traces of Ken Anderson's early story treatments that can be found in The Haunted Mansion's final design, a variety of characters, settings, and situations from each version of the attraction made it into the screenplay. There is the use of the Gracey name and a secret involving Gracey's long-lost love, Elizabeth. There is a wedding that was not meant to be, much like the legend of Phantom Manor, and a pivotal event that occurs during a lavish ball in the mansion's grand hall, just as in all the attractions. In the film, Madame Leota now plays a major role, acting as a tour guide to the supernatural world in which Jim finds himself. And more than a few familiar faces pop up as Jim and his children race through the Gracey family graveyard aboard a runaway hearse. There was definitely going to be a strong sense of déjà vu for longtime fans of the attraction.

Another similarity to the attraction was the screenplay's skillful blend of comedy and horror, uniting Marc Davis's and Claude Coats's visions of the story just as seamlessly on-screen as they did at Disneyland more than thirty years earlier. "You want to make it scary, you want to make it funny," David says. "We thought the best approach would be a combination of both."

David had a challenge familiar to any writer who has been charged with adapting a well-known property, whether it is a novel, TV show, or theme park attraction, into a movie. It's important to retain enough of what is loved about the original while making all the additions and subtractions necessary to enable the material to work as a feature film. The studio executives all agreed that he had nailed it. "David turned in the script and we gave it to Nina on a Friday," Andrew Gunn recalls. "She called me on *Sunday* and said, 'We should make this.'" Dick Cook, chairman of The Walt Disney Studios, quickly agreed, and the search began for talent on both sides of the camera that could bring the mansion and its inhabitants to life.

TOP LEFT: The Hitchhiking Ghosts make a cameo appearance, as seen in these storyboards by Jack Hsu, depicting the Evers family's madcap hearse ride through the Gracey family cemetery. **LEFT:** Shooting the hearse sequence against a blue screen.

RETURN OF THE KING

The studio team recognized that The Haunted Mansion was an important part of their Disney heritage and wanted to entrust it to a production team who felt similarly. They had also been looking for a property to reunite the team that brought *The Lion King* to the world, producer Don Hahn and co-director Rob Minkoff, and hoped both men would want to re-establish their winning partnership.

"I first saw the script in January of 2002, the same one that went to Eddie Murphy," Don recalls. "Then Dick Cook called me and asked if I would be interested in producing *The Haunted Mansion* and working with Rob Minkoff again. It was a fateful coincidence because though I hadn't seen Rob in years, I coincidentally had a lunch scheduled with him the next day! I brought Rob a copy of the script, and the next thing you know, we met with Dick and got running.

"I have a great appreciation for all things Disney," Don continues. "I grew up near the park and The Haunted Mansion was one of my favorite rides. I can vividly remember before it opened that long period of time when the outside was done but the inside wasn't, so the gates weren't open yet. I was just drooling for the day when you could run through those gates and see what the heck was inside. It made a huge impression on me."

"We had been wanting to bring Rob Minkoff back into the Disney family for quite a while," Nina Jacobson says, "and thought this project was the perfect opportunity. He was perfect for the tone we wanted for this movie." After the blockbuster success of *The Lion King*, Minkoff had gone on to direct the two *Stuart Little* films, both of which took advantage of his background in feature animation and proved him more than capable of handling live action.

"I was already a huge fan of the attraction," says Rob, "and there were many times when I was on the ride that I felt it would be a really cool movie. Getting this chance was a great opportunity to realize that, plus I knew it would be absolutely terrific to work with Don again."

Don Hahn officially came on board as producer in March 2002, quickly followed by Rob Minkoff's ascent into the director's chair. Their affection for the attraction ensured that they would remain as faithful to the

ABOVE: Director Rob Minkoff in a grave position. **LEFT:** Minkoff sets the scene on *The Haunted Mansion* set.

Although not used in the movie, the Corridor of Doors came to life in an early test scene directly based on a piece of Claude Coats's concept art.

source material as possible while serving the script. The project would need to stand on its own and work as a film first and foremost, but they didn't want to disappoint the Mansion's millions of fans, who would come to the film with certain expectations. As fans themselves, Don and Rob were determined to meet those expectations.

"There were certain things from the attraction that we knew had to be in there," says Don. "Iconic things that you at least want to pay homage to in the movie, even if they're not part of the plot, like the ballroom dancers, a corridor of doors, or a raven on a tree branch. Many of the characters you're familiar with from the cemetery make cameo appearances. I think the audience will really appreciate that level of detail.

"But there were also pieces of the attraction that had no purpose except to connect the movie back to the ride, which wasn't a good enough reason to use them in the story. For example, we tried to figure out a way for the Stretching Room to make sense in the storytelling but we just couldn't do it. Once we figured out what the story would be, it was important to keep it focused and remain true to the characters we had created.

"The movie needed to stand on its own, but remember that a lot of the Disneyland rides are based on movies," Don continues. "So we had to figure out if the movie should look like it came *after* the attraction or *before* the attraction. We felt it was important for the movie to appear as though it came before the attraction so it had its own integrity, its own sensibility, and its own story. And maybe, after you see the

movie, you'll go back to see the attraction and it'll take on a slightly different meaning."

Disney and ghost movies go hand in hand, from *The Skeleton Dance* and 1937's *Lonesome Ghosts* starring "ghost exterminators" Mickey, Donald, and Goofy, to Ichabod Crane and the Headless Horseman. Don loved all those movies. "I figured if we could tell a story about a family that spends one horrific night in The Haunted Mansion, we'd really be doing something," he states. "But the inspiration is more important than a literal interpretation," Don adds. "We weren't slavish to The Haunted Mansion but slavish to the *spirit* of The Haunted Mansion—no pun intended. It wasn't important to just make a movie of the ride because you can go to the parks and *ride* the ride. We wanted to make a movie that celebrates a whole genre of moviemaking—the haunted house movie."

"As well as making a haunted house movie, there was a fairy tale aspect to the story, a Romeo and Juliet angle," Rob Minkoff says. "It also has the comic elements of the ghosts and Madame Leota, and the adventure and scares that you have out in the mausoleum and the cemetery. It's fun to draw from all these different sources and genres and combine them into something new and different that we haven't seen before."

"It's a very interesting combination," Don reaffirms. "It's a little comedy, a little love story, a little scary, a little bit of a murder mystery, all hung on a very strong fairy tale spine. With zombies," he finishes with a smile.

MURPHY'S LAW

In early 2002, *The Haunted Mansion* started gaining serious momentum at The Walt Disney Studios and some serious buzz in Hollywood. Shortly before Don Hahn and Rob Minkoff signed on, Dick Cook received a phone call from Jim Wiatt, Eddie Murphy's agent. "We hear you're developing a Haunted Mansion movie and Eddie thinks it would be perfect for him," Wiatt told a happily surprised Cook. As it turned out, Murphy, star of *The Nutty Professor* and *Coming to America*, had been developing his own "old dark house" movie, inspired by an early stand-up comedy routine of his about how African Americans would react in a haunted house. *The Haunted Mansion*, with its name recognition and built-in family audience, fit the bill nicely.

Murphy read the script, loved it, and quickly agreed to star as Jim Evers. The production team was thrilled. They knew Murphy would be perfect as an ordinary man who suddenly finds himself and his family in an extraordinary situation. "Audiences enjoy seeing him play this kind of role in this kind of movie, a comedy that's geared to the family," Rob says of the multitalented actor. Jim Evers was written as a workaholic whose total immersion in his job leads him to neglect his family, and the team knew Eddie's natural likability and accessibility would help make the character a bit more sympathetic. That quality would better enable audiences to identify and empathize with Jim Evers as he is thrust into the incredible and increasingly bizarre environment of the haunted mansion.

With an A-list comedy superstar cast in the lead role, the production team moved forward at a brisk pace. In June 2002, the film officially went into pre-production and Rob and Don assembled the creative team that would help them rebuild The Haunted Mansion on the big screen. Like their lead actor, the heads of key departments all came from the A-list in their respective fields: Production Designer John Myhre, Costume Designer Mona May, Special Makeup Effects Designer Rick Baker, Director of Photography Remi Adefarisan, and Visual Effects Supervisor Jay Redd from Sony Imageworks.

ABOVE: The Evers family—Jim (Eddie Murphy), Sara (Marsha Thomason), Megan (Aree Davis), and Michael (Marc John Jefferies)—arrives at the Mansion. **BELOW:** Jim Evers and his kids stumble into the attic, in this concept sketch by Jim Martin.

MEETING OF THE MINDS

Filmmaking has always been a collaborative process, but John, Mona, Rick, Remi, and Jay enjoyed an especially symbiotic relationship while working on *The Haunted Mansion*. The lines between reality and fantasy, and art and technology, have grown increasingly blurry over the years and these five artists needed to keep in constant contact to ensure that Rick Baker's characters would look right in Mona May's costumes on John Myhre's sets as photographed by Remi Adefarisan. This process didn't end once the images were captured on film. Redd and his visual effects team at Sony

Imageworks digitally added certain elements, such as an eerie blue glow or wispy tendrils of plasmic energy, and subtracted others, such as skin and bones, to complete the ghosts' overall look. "There are things you can do in the CG [computer graphics] realm that we just can't do with makeup, and vice versa," Rick Baker says. "I think this 'marriage' between the two was the best relationship to have with some of these characters. Films are about such a collaboration, and that's one reason why I love this business."

It was also vital that all of these vastly different entities, from genuinely gruesome reanimated corpses to the more cartoonish inhabitants of the graveyard to purely digital floating phantoms, all feel as though they are part of the same "reality."

"A zombie scene was added to the movie and they wanted fairly realistic, very skeletal zombies," Rick recalls. "I was afraid of what it would do to the tone of the film, with stylized ghosts over here and realistic zombies over there. We had to make it all work in the same movie."

ABOVE: Rick Baker (**LEFT**), decked out as a Marc Davis-inspired happy haunt, has some chilling advice for Visual Effects Supervisor Jay Redd; **LEFT:** The creative minds of (**LEFT TO RIGHT**) Producer Don Hahn, Director Rob Minkoff, Costume Designer Mona May, Supervising Art Director Tomas Voth, and Production Designer John Myhre meet on the set.

"The biggest challenge was to keep each element working with each other, so it didn't feel like you were watching separate movies," Mona agrees. "There had to be a common thread so the graveyard didn't feel separate from the Mardi Gras or the zombies. Even though they change, the mood, the colors, and the textures had unity."

"You want everything to look different but similar enough so you know that it's coming from the same supernatural world," Jay concurs. If even one character felt out of place, the film's continuity and the audience's willing suspension of disbelief would both be threatened. Only through constant communication could the artists ensure that those seams would remain invisible. Their work is a testament to the power of collaboration, with ancient art forms joining forces with twenty-first-century technology to create the film's incredible illusions and bring its other-worldly cast of characters to life on-screen.

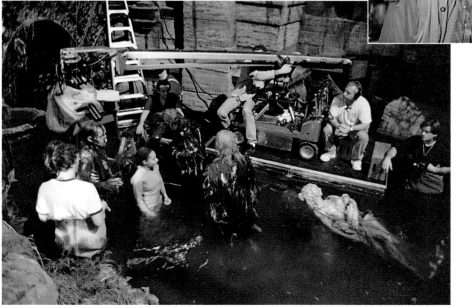

TOP LEFT: Location Manager Ralph Coleman (**RIGHT**) discusses sites for the Evers house with (**LEFT TO RIGHT**) Rob, Don, and Executive Producer Barry Bernardi. **TOP RIGHT, AND LEFT:** The crew setting up to shoot on the mausoleum set. **ABOVE:** The director shares his vision as Eddie Murphy gets into character.

This New Old House

ROB MINKOFF QUICKLY BEGAN meeting with his department heads to share his vision of the film. Though there would be moments of B-movie horror and broad comedy, he wanted the project's overall look to have a high level of class and sophistication that audiences might not expect from such a "popcorn movie." He called it "haunted elegance," a phrase that perfectly captured the unique blend of Gothic horror, romance, fantasy, and refinement that he was seeking. "Each film has its own unique style" Rob says. "The visual style has to be appropriate for the material and the story you're telling. I wanted a richness of texture and detail that really informed the storytelling."

"I think I was a kindred spirit with Rob and Don, being a fan of the attraction at Disneyland since I was a little kid," says Production Designer John Myhre. "I thought the idea of doing something with one of the attractions was really terrific and, to me, The Haunted Mansion was the best one of all." The Academy Award–winning veteran of period pieces such as *Chicago* and blockbuster genre films like *X-Men*, John looked forward to the challenge of finding a home for 999 happy haunts.

John not only needed to design a mansion that would instantly recall the attraction and work on the big screen at the same time, but he also had to reinterpret Claude Coats and company's richly detailed interiors. From the Conservatory and Séance Circle to the Grand Hall and the Graveyard, some of the attraction's key locations were every bit as memorable as its story line and characters. He also needed to create all-new environments unique to the film. His designs for new areas such as the mansion's great Entrance Hall, Armory, and elaborate French–Gothic Mausoleum all feel as though they are a part of that same world and

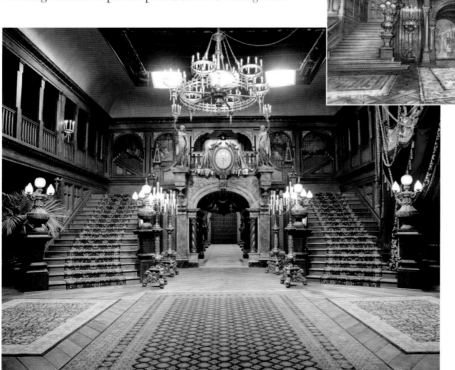

The mansion's great Entrance Hall, from sketch (**ABOVE**) to reality (**LEFT**). **OPPOSITE TOP:** The evolution of the Grand Hall, as seen in a piece of concept art (**TOP**), a technical rendering (**RIGHT**), and a scale model (**LEFT**). **OPPOSITE BOTTOM:** Production Designer John Myhre on a finished set.

always have been. Familiar motifs are also apparent, such as watching eyes; and new ones, such as draped figures, have been added.

The production design team drew their inspiration from a wide variety of cinematic, literary, and artistic sources. The walls of the production offices were lined with inspirational art and photographs from countless films, from *The Old Dark House* and *The Cat and the Canary* to *The Uninvited* and *The Haunting* (the 1963 original that influenced Claude Coats). For certain locations in and around the mansion, they even looked at Roger Corman's Edgar Allan Poe pictures and William Castle's kitschy B-movies of the 1960s. In an effort to recall as much of the original attraction's interior design as possible, original Imagineering conceptual art and still photographs of the sets could

TOP AND ABOVE: The set for Séance Circle and in concept art.
RIGHT AND BELOW: A new location, the Armory, takes its
place alongside established Haunted Mansion environments.

also be found throughout their studio. The two houses would not be identical twins, but they would at least be first cousins. No gravestone was left unturned in the search for supernaturally inspirational imagery.

"Part of the fun was that each room could have a bit of a different architectural flair," John says. "I started grabbing references from really opulent, wonderful places, because this was a house that was put together, in a way, almost the way [William Randolph] Hearst did, where one room would be one style, another room would be another style, with huge fireplaces from Italy and wallpaper from somewhere else. . . ."

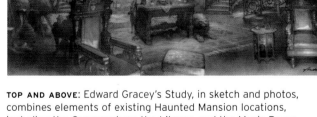

TOP AND ABOVE: Edward Gracey's Study, in sketch and photos, combines elements of existing Haunted Mansion locations, including the Conservatory, the Library, and the Music Room. **BELOW**: Details of props placed throughout the Study set.

"NAILING" THE HOUSE

One of the biggest challenges was designing the look of the exterior of the house. Although the film was never intended to be a direct lift of the attraction, the production team knew that fans would be expecting a house that in some way resembled either the Mansion at Disneyland or one of its sister parks. Early drafts of the script were set in upstate New York, which suggested a design along the lines of the Dutch Gothic manor house seen at Walt Disney World and Tokyo Disneyland. After the location changed to New Orleans, the team considered a look similar to that of the iconic Addams Family–style mansion, which was not dissimilar to the old house on the hill in the first Harper Goff sketch from 1951. A scouting trip to Disneyland, however, convinced John once and for all that his design should be based on the Park's antebellum mansion. Using the Disneyland design as a starting point, John and his team began to create a mansion that would be recognizable to fans and at the same time conform to Rob Minkoff's vision of haunted elegance.

"When everyone decided on the Southern-style house," says John, "I visited many of the mansions around New Orleans. They turned out to be quite small in comparison to what our story required,

ABOVE: Concept illustrator Nathan Schroeder created many different images of the mansion, including this exterior view (**TOP**).

usually only two stories tall, in a nice, prim shape and painted white. They were very romantic. We, on the other hand, wanted something that felt haunted and mysterious."

As they began their designs, John and his team quickly realized that the 999 haunts also needed to be lodged in much larger accomodations. The mansion needed to be ominous, intimidating, and tower above anyone who dared to approach. The increase in the mansion's size led to the deletion of one of the Disneyland version's most recognizable features—its great marble columns. "Once marble columns go higher than two stories," John explains, "you no longer have a quaint Southern mansion—you have a government building like the White House." Taking his cue from the

New Orleans location, Myhre replaced the problematic pillars with much thinner, wrought-iron versions, recalling the grace of the French Quarter and playing even better to Minkoff's concept of haunted elegance. "I thought instead of doing the traditional house with stone columns, it would be fun to use wrought iron," John adds. "It made the house look really skinny, almost like the whole thing could fall over at any point. It became a motif of the film."

Walt's decree that they'd take care of the outside and the ghosts would take care of the inside was happily confined to Disneyland. The big screen version needed to look like a truly haunted mansion, and John's team responded with a crumbling stone edifice that looked ready to fall in on itself, a rotting hulk that was practically sinking into the bayou it overlooked. This approach also changed the mansion's color palette, giving it more of a greenish tint, thanks to hundreds of years of exposure to the elements deep in bayou country, as opposed to the cream-white hue at Disneyland. In a nod to the Walt Disney World design, a great wrought-iron-and-glass conservatory was attached to the right side of the house, the setting for a number of the film's key scenes.

In its final version, the mansion appears to be a direct descendant of the Disneyland original (or perhaps an ancestor, according to the filmmakers), suitably expanded and enhanced to work on the big screen. With its isolated location on the edge of a Louisiana bayou, the house also possessed a distinctly Gothic feel, a forbidding, remote environment that was perfect for the tale of forbidden love that David Berenbaum had crafted.

ABOVE AND BOTTOM LEFT: Front and side views of the mansion façade. **BELOW:** Detail of the estate's wrought-iron entrance gate. **BOTTOM:** Lion's head door knocker.

TOP: Production Designer John Myhre and his team built the first forty feet of the mansion on the edge of a man-made "bayou" at Sable Ranch. The red balloon floating above marks the top of the mansion's cupola, which was computer generated and added in post production. **ABOVE LEFT:** A computer rendering of the mansion's roofline and signature cupola. **ABOVE RIGHT:** Director of Photography Remi Adefarasin sets up a shot on location with Director Rob Minkoff. **RIGHT:** A rough composite of the mansion's exterior facade and its computer-generated upper floors was used for reference while shooting on location. **OPPOSITE BOTTOM:** These test shots, with Eddie Murphy and Marsha Thomason, show the mansion before and after the cupola has been digitally added.

LOCATION, LOCATION, LOCATION

Once Minkoff and company decided what kind of house they were going to build, they had to find a good neighborhood. Location shooting in New Orleans itself would have been cost-prohibitive, so the mansion's exterior and the adjacent graveyard were constructed on the grounds of Sable Ranch, located deep in Southern California's canyon country.

"Sable Ranch was perfect," Rob declares. "There were a number of dead trees in the area where we built the house. There was an area called Oak Alley filled with oaks where we did the cemetery sets. There was also a clay bed that could retain water." The house was built on the edge of the clay bed, which was then filled with water to create a man-made bayou. All that needed to be added was a little Spanish moss to the property's towering trees.

John Myhre and his crew built an imposing structure, which stood close to forty feet tall and comprised roughly half the house. The rest of the mansion's upper floors, another forty feet's worth including its signature cupola, were created digitally in post production by Jay Redd and his crew at Imageworks. "We needed something to mark the top of the cupola as a reference point," John recalls. "Every idea proposed was incredibly expensive, such as a crane rising almost a hundred feet in the air. Finally someone suggested getting a red balloon and tying it to a string. So that's what we used—which cost us $7.87, compared to $2,000 a day for a crane!" This solution could be considered an unknowing nod to Imagineers, who use balloons to mark the tops of attractions during construction to get a sense of how they will fit in with the rest of the park.

A second film unit traveled to Savannah, Georgia, which stood in for New Orleans, to shoot footage for the Evers family's drive into bayou country. In the final film, audiences would never know that the crew had never set foot in the Crescent City.

The mansion under construction on location at Sable Ranch.

THE STAGE IS SET

With construction on the mansion's exterior underway at Sable Ranch, the production set up shop at Barwick Studios in Glendale, just a fifteen-minute drive from The Walt Disney Studios in Burbank. Unlike many film productions, which have sets and even entire departments scattered across Southern California, *The Haunted Mansion* team was able to house its entire crew and build all its interior sets at the Barwick Studios. If Rob Minkoff needed to consult with John Myhre or approve one of Mona May's designs, they were just down the hall. Even Rick Baker's Cinovation Studios was just a five-minute drive away.

Just downstairs from the production offices, Barwick's soundstages were home to the first Haunted Mansion sets built outside a Disney theme park. Every one of John Myhre's elaborate interior sets were built on-site, from the cavernous Grand Hall to the ornate interior of the Gracey family mausoleum, which was flooded with water for the Evers family's subterranean encounter with an army of zombies. With the production's headquarters just up the stairs, for the cast and crew of *The Haunted Mansion*, there really was no place like home.

Clothes Make the Corpse

OSTUME DESIGNER MONA MAY's credits include the costumes for *Clueless*, which were not only a highlight of the film but also had a major influence on the fashion world, as well as *Romy and Michele's High School Reunion* and *Stuart Little 2*, for Rob Minkoff. "I dressed the mouse," Mona recalls, "and that was an interesting prelude to this film because the mouse doesn't really exist. It's only a digital character. So already I was familiar with designing for a phantom."

Ultimately, the project would require her to design a variety of costumes that encompassed such a broad timeline, it was similar to designing four or five different films concurrently. In addition to creating the wardrobe for the film's modern-day "human" characters, Mona also needed to dress eighteenth-century Mardi Gras masquerade ball guests and ghosts spanning multiple geographical regions and historical periods, not to mention a small army of flesh-hungry zombies and rotting corpses.

Mona needed to figure out how to redress her creepy cast while remaining true to the source material. Additionally, according to the "ghost logic" the team was slowly developing for the film, the physical appearance of the ghosts would change depending on whether they were inside the mansion, out in the graveyard, or, in the case of the zombies that Jim Evers and his kids encounter inside the mausoleum, in the ground or a coffin. The job was clearly going to involve a little more than ordering some translucent raincoats, the ghosts' typical raiment in the original Haunted Mansion attraction.

"All sorts of questions were put on the table regarding the ghosts," says Mona. "How much of the ghosts do we see? How white are their faces? How real are their clothes? Would they have a fuzz around them? Would they have a glow? As we worked on our sketches, we kept getting closer and closer to the answers."

ABOVE: Costume Designer Mona May adjusting her *haunt* couture. **LEFT AND BELOW:** Costume sketches of Ezra the Footman (Wallace Shawn), Emma the Maid (Dina Waters), and Ramsley the Butler (Terence Stamp) by Felipe Sanchez.

Concept designs of Elizabeth's wedding dress (BELOW) and Mardi Gras costume (RIGHT) by Mona May, sketched by Felipe Sanchez.

LEFT: May's costume design, complete with fabric swatches, for Nathaniel Parker as Edward Gracey. ABOVE: Costume designs for Terence Stamp's Ramsley the Butler and Edward Gracey.

The "swinging wake" becomes a Mardi Gras ball, as seen in these samples of costume design by Mona May, rendered by Felipe Sanchez, and production stills from the film.

Mona drew her inspiration from scores of films, art books, historical texts, print ads, and fashion photography. Open-minded to all sources, she looked at the floating movements of sea anemones and the glowing, incorporeal feel of semitransparent deep-sea creatures. She also took visual cues from the edgy "Goth" look and from an ethereal and vaguely otherworldly style in fashion that had started appearing as the movie commenced production. "Ripped, ghostly, textury stuff was starting to become very 'in' when I began my designs, which was quite interesting," Mona says with a laugh. "We were obviously in vibe with the trendsetters." The result is an eclectic collection of costumes complemented by equally bold hair and makeup designs, helping to create what is perhaps the most sophisticated assortment of ghosts, ghouls, and goblins ever captured on film.

It was important to Rob Minkoff that his ghosts look distinctly different from the other apparitions seen in countless films over the years, and Mona would play a crucial role in developing that look. One of the ways in which her costumes helped make their ghosts unique was their shimmering, iridescent quality.

"We used tiny, almost microscopic spherical mirrors manufactured by 3M, called 'Scotchlite,' on the costumes," Visual Effects Supervisor Jay Redd recalls. "It's what's used on running shoes, jogging suits, and freeway signs to make them visible at night, because the light that goes toward the mirrored bead reflects right back to the source. It's the same effect that your car headlights have on freeway signs, making them visible a mile away. These tiny mirrors were added to paint and put on the costumes. Working with Remi Adefarasin, the director of photography, we devised a way to put a 'headlight' mounted directly onto the camera, right at the lens. When the camera points at a reflective bead-painted costume, a beautiful, ethereal, and ghostly effect is produced. Then we took this photography into Visual Effects and used the bright reflections and glows to create a smoky, otherworldly floating energy. This energy effect was then run in reverse to create an even more supernatural look."

ABOVE: The Graveyard Opera Singer slims down a bit and tries on a new outfit, as seen in Mona May's costume design for "Brunhilde." **BELOW:** May's designs join with Jay Redd's effects to create a look based on the creative team's "ghost logic." **(LEFT TO RIGHT)** Actor in costume with reflective paint effect; extracted ghost with particle energy effect; plasmic energy and smoke elements; the final composite test image with added glow, smoke, and light effects.

On-screen, costumes covered with these microscopic glass beads—and thus the ghosts themselves—appear to give off a twinkling, supernatural glow in a way that had never been seen before on film. This unique "glass-wear" was just one of the many ways in which Mona May's costume design contributed to the distinctive look that Minkoff and his team desired.

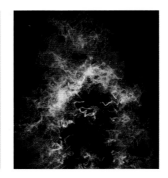

The New Man of a Thousand Faces

T HE PRODUCTION TEAM KNEW that one of the most important elements in a movie entitled *The Haunted Mansion* would be the ghosts themselves, 999 of them in this case. Much like that of the house itself, the look of the infamous "happy haunts" would need to recall the attraction's classic character designs as well as satisfy a sophisticated twenty-first-century film audience. In an age when filmmakers can conjure up almost anything inside a computer, Rob Minkoff felt that having "real" and not computer-generated ghosts would feel much more natural and organic. For that they hired what they considered to be an ace in the hole, Special Makeup Effects Designer Rick Baker.

A true master of his craft, Baker had worked his unique brand of magic on some of the greatest genre films in movie history, including *Star Wars*, *Men in Black*, and *An American Werewolf in London*, for which he won the first Academy Award for Makeup. Rick had worked with Eddie Murphy before, transforming the comedian into *The Nutty Professor*, as well as virtually every other member of the Klump family.

Much like Don Hahn and Rob Minkoff, it was Rick's own lifelong love of The Haunted Mansion that

attracted him to the project, and he was not at all intimidated by the prospect of tinkering with a pop cultural classic. After all, Baker was no stranger to "re-imagining" characters audiences already knew and loved, including the Grinch, the Incredible Hulk, and the simian inhabitants of the *Planet of the Apes*.

"The studio didn't want to just go the CG [computer graphics] route with the ghosts," Rick recalls, "and called me. There really is something to be said for having characters that are actually there on the day of shooting, with the same light in the same environment.

"So they asked if I was interested, and of course I said yes. I love The Haunted Mansion. We got to walk through it with all the lights on—that was reason enough to do this! Plus I love working with Eddie Murphy even though he's one of the few characters without makeup."

Baker signed on in April 2002 and immediately went to work designing makeup for Edward Gracey, the butler Ramsley, and the motley assortment of ghosts, ghouls, skeletons, and zombies who haunt the house and grounds. Throughout the spring and summer, he produced a series of conceptual sketches, paintings, maquettes, and sculptures of all the key characters and supporting players. Rick knew that his designs would have to serve the story of the film and not stray too far from the original characters that audiences knew and loved. With that in mind, Marc Davis's original sketches and concept art began dotting the walls of Rick's studio to inspire him as he adapted virtually all of Davis's creations for leading, supporting, and cameo roles in the film, including Madame Leota, a variety of Grand Hall party guests, the Attic's "pop-up" ghosts, Graveyard musicians and revelers, and, of course, the ubiquitous Hitchhiking Ghosts.

The film offered a broad canvas on which to paint, so Rick set himself free to play, creating designs for completely original characters to complement the cast from the attraction. "The fun part was coming up with all sorts of creative ways for them to have died," Rick says with a gleeful grin. He made a conscious attempt to emulate the design intent of his Imagineering predecessors, and many of his new characters look as though they have leaped off Marc Davis's drawing board. His own happy haunts include a snake charmer who drew his cobra a little too far out of its basket, a deep-sea diver wearing an octopus in addition to a helmet, and a William Tell disciple with an apple on his head and an arrow in his forehead.

OPPOSITE: The Mausoleum zombies playfully turn on their creator, Special Makeup Effects Designer Rick Baker.
TOP: Hitchhiking Ghost "Phineas" and a graveyard pal played by Rick Baker.

ABOVE: Rick Baker and Bill Corso put the finishing touches on Hitchhiker Jeremy Howard. **BELOW:** Baker stayed very true to Marc Davis's original designs for *The Haunted Mansion*'s Hitchhiking Ghosts, as seen in this striking concept art.

Ghost Logic

ALTHOUGH ROB MINKOFF relied on live actors and Rick Baker's makeup designs to bring most of the ghosts to life, he knew that state-of-the-art visual effects would play a vital role during post production. For that he turned to Visual Effects Supervisor Jay Redd, a veteran of the movies *Babe*, *Contact*, and both *Stuart Little* films, and Producer Lynda Thompson, who had worked on a number of Disney films dating back to *Tron* in 1982.

Jay and his team contributed heavily to the development of the project's "ghost logic," the rules that governed the appearance and physical (as well as not-so-physical) attributes of the spirits inside the mansion and outside in the cemetery. After lengthy discussions between Jay, Rob, and screenwriter David Berenbaum, it was determined that the ghosts would look and behave differently depending on whether they were inside or outside the house. "We didn't want to create the stereotypical, green and blue floaty ghosts that you see in other horror movies," Redd recalls. "We wanted to do something completely different, so we came up with this whole idea of 'ghost logic.' We had to define not only the rules of their existence, such as *why* they exist, but *how* they exist—what visual characteristics they would take on." The ghosts that Jim Evers and his kids encounter in the graveyard, for example, would only be visible when viewed through the windows of the ghostly horse-drawn hearse. This logic stemmed from the idea that the house and its inhabitants are cursed to be trapped inside the confines of the mansion or objects associated with the mansion, much like a bird in a cage. As long as a ghost stays inside the mansion, he or she appears normal to living humans, with an ability to interact with Jim and his family. However, if a ghost leaves the house, he or she would lose the ability to appear as "normal", and would instead take on a supernatural and somewhat scary look, frightening anyone away that might want to associate with them. Thus, the curse's promise is fulfilled—an eternity of loneliness and no escape. This is why Emma and Ezra appear "ghostly" outside the house—they have attempted to break from the curse.

"It was a great challenge to jump into visualizing something that can't be seen," Jay continues. "It gave us a clean slate to create something really magical, but we still had to establish some rules. In creating our 'ghost logic' we had to treat the whole idea in a legitimate and almost scientific manner." The filmmakers knew that in order to create a believable world of The

ABOVE AND OPPOSITE: Various computer-generated elements, including bones, skin, and plasmic energy, make up just one frame of the completed illusion of a ghostly horse. **BELOW:** Visual Effects Supervisor Jay Redd.

Haunted Mansion, certain consistencies would have to be invented and retained in order to make sense of the supernatural visual effects that appear on screen.

Says Jay on the ghost look, "All things are essentially made up energy. I think the ghosts are full of the same amount of energy as living humans, but they're now on a different physical plane, with the energy organized in a different manner. It's just like the light above your dinner table is the same as the lightning in a storm—they're both electricity—or like sand on the beach is really the same material as a glass bottle.

"We all have our own self-image," he continues, "and the ghosts are no different. The ghosts still have an image of themselves, just as you and I do. As an apparition, you still want to be seen as yourself. They exist as an impression of their once-living selves, only this time in a much more unstable manner. The physical parts of the ghosts that were buried, such as clothes or jewelry, might take on a more solid appearance, because they still exist in the real world. But the flesh, the brain, and the heart, anything that was living—all of that stuff's gone.

"Another concept is that ghosts aren't able to get their energy from eating, sleeping, and physical activity, such as we do. In talking with Rob, I came up with the idea that the ghosts would 'steal' their energy from their surroundings, pulling energy away from the environment they're in—the grass, the trees, the stones. As a ghost, I may be unorganized energy, but I would still have a 'core energy.' This is the soul."

GHOSTS IN THE MACHINE

Jay and his team created the ethereal trails of ectoplasm and crackles of electrical energy around the ghosts' "bodies." "We started with Mona May's costumed actors with makeup effects from Rick Baker's team, and we filmed them against a blue screen," explains Jay. "These ghosts have the reflective paint on their costumes, giving a special never-before-seen iridescent, reflective effect. We took this photography, scanned it into the digital realm, and began their supernatural transformation. We added special glows, changed transparency, and added particle and digital smoke effects to create the 'core' or 'soul' of the ghost. This energy comes from the center of the once-living body, and emanates outward to form the ethereal torso, arms, and legs. On the outside of the body, we added plasmic tendrils, wispy smoke trails, and more electrical energy pops, and ran them all in

reverse to create the 'energy stealing' effects. They really are haunting, elegant, and beautiful at the same time." Imageworks' artists and programmers wrote special software to create the ghosts' glowing and vibrant colors, to allow integration with all of the other digital effects applied. All of these custom-designed processes distinguish the ghosts from the many blue and gray, transparent entities seen in films throughout the years.

Some of the happy haunts in the story weren't ghosts at all, but reanimated corpses treated as actual physical beings that behaved differently from their spiritual siblings. These zombies were actually right

there on the set, buried beneath Rick Baker's makeup and Mona May's tattered costumes. Then the visual effects artists digitally erased pieces of skin and bone to further enhance the illusion that the corpses were rotting away to nothing.

A few of the happy haunts were one hundred-percent completely computer-generated, most notably the wispy spirits and banshees that streak through the graveyard. Where Yale Gracey and Rolly Crump used simple projection effects to raise their spirits, Jay Redd and his crew designed and created special software to create the restless wraiths that streak through the night sky on their way to a midnight jamboree.

Jay and his crew used motion control photography to create the illusion that there were swarms of zombies in the mausoleum, instead of just the fifteen that Rick Baker created for the film. A computerized camera was programming to perform the same move the same way every time the camera was turned on. Rick's fifteen zombies would be positioned in a particular section, or "slice" of the circular mausoleum, much like dividing up a pie. The camera would then perform the programmed move, film the specific inhabited section, then the zombies were moved to a different slice, mixed up, and then filmed again. This process was performed for six or eight slices, then scanned and composited at Imageworks to create the illusion of dozens of zombies attacking Jim and his daughter.

OPPOSITE TOP: Madame Leota gives Jim Evers a lift during the shooting of their first meeting in the Séance Room. **ABOVE AND TOP:** A restless zombie has a bone to pick with Jim Evers in the subterranean mausoleum. **OPPOSITE BOTTOM AND BELOW:** Jennifer Tilly is filmed first against a blue screen; then her image is combined with a raw background plate and various smoke, energy, and lighting effects to create the "quiet storm" inside Leota's crystal ball before uniting into a final test composite of all the elements.

RICK BAKER © '02

The Transformation Is Complete

WITH THE RELEASE OF THE MOVIE, The Haunted Mansion has literally come full circle. It was born in 1951, when a movie art director named Harper Goff became one of the first Imagineers and drew a sketch of a sinister Victorian mansion. Years later Walt Disney first spoke of a retirement home for ghosts. Ken Anderson picked up the project and established the Mansion's look and a number of its key characters and story points. Then Yale Gracey and Rolly Crump formed a creative partnership, producing illusions and special effects that would have little equal even a half century later. Marc Davis, Claude Coats, and X. Atencio picked up the baton and crafted a legend that lives on not only at Disneyland but also at three other Magic Kingdoms around the world, in defiance of national and cultural boundaries. More than fifty years after that first little sketch, a new generation of talented filmmakers told the story yet again, this time in the medium that inspired so many of the theme park attractions: the motion picture.

The Haunted Mansion story is not likely to end here. Walt Disney once said "Disneyland will never be completed . . . as long as there is imagination left in the world." The same can be said of the old dark house on the hill. The Haunted Mansion has made a fifty-year journey from the Magic Kingdom to the movies,

OPPOSITE: Rick Baker's concept painting of Jennifer Tilly as Madame Leota. **THIS PAGE:** Imagineers have developed a number of new concepts for The Haunted Mansion over the years, including an enhancement in which two ghosts grapple with a secret panel (**ABOVE**), additional special effects for the Corridor of Doors (**BELOW RIGHT**), and an elaborate redesign of the load area (**BELOW LEFT**). You never know when they just might *materialize.*

and there's no telling where it will go in the next fifty. Only Madame Leota knows for sure, but The Haunted Mansion will likely relocate again as technologies and new media develop, as long as there is imagination left in the world.